**Kerry Trent Haggard
&
Johnny Dale Cochran II**

First edition published in 2018 by Flying Disk Press

FLYING DISK PRESS
4 St Michaels Avenue
Pontefract
West Yorkshire
England
WF8 4QX

Published by FLYING DISK PRESS

Cover design by Mark Randall

Chapters

"Holy cats…We finally got one! We've found a flying saucer!"

Howard Hawks' classic film
"The Thing From Another World"
1951

"My God... I see people in this thing!"

Last radio transmission before the crash of
Kentucky Air National Guardsman Captain
Thomas Mantell as he attempted to intersect
a large slow moving UFO. January 7, 1948

"The nations of the world will have to unite, for the next war will be an interplanetary war. The nations of the earth must someday make a common front against attack by people from other planets."

General Douglas MacArthur
New York Times interview, 1955

*"I'd like to tell the public about the alien situation...
but my hands are tied."*

J.F.K., summer 1963

"These babies are huge, sir… Enormous… Oh God, you wouldn't believe it! I'm telling you there are other spacecraft out here… Lined up on the far side of the crater edge…They're on the moon… watching us!"

Colonel Edwin "Buzz" Aldrin
Apollo 11 mission July 1969

"Hello Houston, this is Discovery. We still have the alien spacecraft under observation."

Transmission from Shuttle Discovery to Houston Control
March 13, 1989

Introduction

"Traveler"

is a two fold story. The 1897 sections are based on documented historical facts detailing the Aurora, Texas single alien crash in the early morning of April 17th, 1897. Written in the past tense, they are, however, my own interpretation of how the actual events may have played out in the old west at the close of the 19th century. I tried to imagine how the good people of a small south-western town may react to such an unprecedented happening. How they may deal with and comprehend the phenomenon of an honest to goodness extraterrestrial craft falling from the heavens in a time when nothing but birds ruled the sky. How they may come together to cope with such an occurrence and its aftermath not only physically but mentally and how it would go down in their history.

Reported in both the *Dallas Morning News* and *Fort Worth Observer*, stories concerning the event were subsequently handed down from elders of the time. Some accounts swore it was the most astonishing thing to have ever happened in the community. Others claimed it was all a lie, made up to try and save a town that was in serious trouble due to fire, crop failure and epidemic.

The good people of Aurora today must feel certain the story is true. In the local cemetery there is an official monument detailing the graveyard's history which mentions the event. Placed there by the Texas Historical Commission in 1976, the inscription concerning the alien is as follows, "*This site is also well known because of the legend that a spaceship crashed nearby in 1897 and the pilot, killed in the crash, was buried here."*

Taken from real life occurrences and situations from our vastly different pasts for the purpose of creating this novel and screenplay, the 1997 sections written in the present tense were created by Odessa, Texas native, Johnny Cochran and I during the summer of 2015. The two backgrounds combined tell some pretty wild accounts to give the reader an entertaining fictional tale based on a substantial historical event.

Many of the stories included in this work such as the railroad tie thrown in the road, the angry Pomeranian locked in the van, the misguided hand grenade and the visit from the reptiles truly took place!

Most works of this type come together in a certain order. First the book, then the screenplay. Not so in this case. Not saying that *Traveler* came together in the wrong order, let's just say it came together backwards. After writing the story in the format for a feature film, then rewriting and refining it dozens of times afterwards, I went back and began to expand the story as well as the backgrounds of characters there in without time restraints for the format of a book.

The 1897 Aurora event hit me with such strong enthusiasm; it was the golden opportunity to write a tale stemming from my personal passion with the UFO phenomenon. It was the early '70, collectively known as *"The Great UFO Wave of 1973."* A surge of unidentified flying object sightings occurred throughout the United States that year including where I was born and raised in a little Northeast Georgia town named Commerce. The events were so talked about, they made newspaper headlines around the state from Athens to Valdosta and several local Atlanta station's TV News. A three man television crew out of Georgia's capitol observed and captured several minutes of footage showing a strange bright colored hovering object on September 9th. That same month President elect Jimmy Carter filled out his own official UFO report, a 1969 evening event in which he and a group of 20 others witnessed strange green lights in the western sky which grew brighter before disappearing.

Unexplained sightings of bizarre lights and a reported landing in June of '73 of a flying saucer in the tiny town of Danielsville (12 miles from our home), had resulted in numerous night time chases by local law officials of fast moving illuminated craft from above. Scenes you would have thought were right out of the imagination of Steven Spielberg's *Close Encounters* in which police cars were wildly chasing after flying saucers.

My ol' man worked as part time radio dispatcher at our Commerce Police Department for 19 years, stopping only when a heart attack he suffered on the job sidelined him in 2000. Regularly interested in the shenanigans of the local *"Keystone Kops"* as he often referred to them, long before taking a position there, a police band radio ran day and night on the small table beside his recliner.

There'd been chatter for weeks on his Realistic brand *"scanner"* from surrounding counties of almost nightly activity concerning mysterious aerial phenomena. Local folks who were phoning in dozens of reports to law officials, of curious lights slowly cruising atop their homes. Close sightings of aerial *"things"* around the area were the talk of the town as well as our small weekly newspaper.

One evening, just past sunset, the P.D. squawk box went crazy as hysterical Commerce residents began reporting low hovering vehicles with bright blinking lights. Coming to a head around 9pm, the on-duty radio dispatcher announced that several callers confirmed a flaming object had sat down somewhere in the vicinity of the Medical Center Clinic. A licensed L.P.N. since 1955, they spoke of the very doctor's office building in which my mother was employed. Hearing the broadcast and begging for her to take me and investigate, I was 9 at the time and didn't have to beg for very long as she was as interested in the bizarre happenings as me. Off we went in my mom's 1968 Oldsmobile green panelled station wagon as fast as we could go! Arriving within minutes half a dozen cars were on the scene, locals who'd heard the same announcements on their radios, in addition to two Commerce Police cruisers and the only fire truck from the local volunteer department.

No, much to all our disappointment there was no "*Thing From Another World*" sitting in the center of the parking lot, but there was something truly astonishing in the far corner. A large discolored smoking circle, 30 feet in diameter and still boiling hot. Along its circumference, small continuous dime size splatters of some unknown silver metal lay as if molten lead had dripped onto the asphalt.   But from what??????

The most vivid memory of my childhood, something large and round in shape had landed, then quickly lifted back off producing great heat in the short time it had taken for frantic calls to pour in police headquarters and our little group to arrive on the scene.   No hoax!   No trick!

This wasn't makeshift crop circles made by some jackass with 2x4s in a farmer's field or a silver painted paper plate dangling from a string in front of a camera. This phenomena had occurred in my little home town and was there right in front of us. From that moment forward, I was a believer in the enigma of *Unidentified Flying Objects*.

Not sure how to react, few that night said anything, they just looked on in amazement for a short while before getting back in their cars and leaving. The officers on scene radioed back to the station that they'd found a sizable burnt circle in the pavement. Nothing more. What else was there to say?

We ventured back the following day to revisit the strange scene, as did dozens of curious thrill seeking members of the community as word of the incident spread.

That was the last time anyone had the opportunity to view or analyze the mysterious odd metallic droppings, now cooled and glittering brightly in the sunshine. The very next day, on a Sunday no less in the Bible belt south when every devout Christian sinner observed the Sabbath and prayed for forgiveness, the entire parking lot was repaved.

Under the cover of darkness that Saturday night, an asphalt crew was quickly and quietly moved in and by the time the good people of Commerce, Georgia were out and about the following morning, all traces of the incident were covered over by several inches of fresh hot black resurfacing material.

"You'll never believe what they did!" I discovered on Monday evening when my mother arrived home from work, *"They repaved the whole parking lot."* Whether or not the hot smoking circle was indeed created by some alien craft touching down in our fair town and taking off again I can not say. But ever since that evening the thing that's disturbed and annoyed me most about what happened so many years ago is who were *they* to decide so quickly to go to such extreme measures to cover up the mystery… and why? Was it drawing too much attention? Was it radioactive?

I doubt it. My suspicion is that it was just one more in an overwhelmingly long list of unexplained events such as this throughout our country where any proof, any trace that we may possibly have been visited by superior intelligent beings from another world has been covered up, or in this case covered over by cowardly and arrogant government officials who continually deny the truth of extraterrestrial travelers to our planet. Who do *they* think they're fooling?

As Fox Mulder believes, *"The truth is out there!!"*

When asked throughout my life, *"Do you believe in extraterrestrials?"* my answer has always been a definitive "Yes!" I, along with millions of others, staunchly believe that we have been visited for thousands of years by superior beings and that the 1947 Roswell, New Mexico flying saucer crash was and remains one of the greatest U.S. government cover-ups of the 20th century. Various places around the world including Europe, Russia and many countries in South America have opened up their UFO files to the public while the U.S. to this day continues to water down, tear apart and falsify the facts in order to remain defiant and deceive its people from the truth. Thankfully, in today's world of non-stop news and YouTube disclosure, influential people from all corners of the globe give their all to expose that same truth.

The fact that the Roswell incident in the summer of '47 remains the most famous doesn't mean the UFO phenomenon began in the 1940s. The impact from extraterrestrial travelers has shaped civilization since prehistoric times. Primitive statues, inscriptions, stone carvings, documents and coins have evolved through history to reveal observations of recurrent contact with non-human visitors who traveled to and from our world.

Historical records from cultures living in all corners of the world tell the same story. In the distant past various *"godlike"* individuals from unknown planetary systems possessing great powers and astounding technology, including the ability to fly with ease, helped to mold mankind into the present form it remains today. Floating craft with mysterious lights have been reported and recorded for posterity throughout the ages.

Ancient inhabitants of cultures worldwide worshiped divine floating angels. Pre-biblical aeronauts and astronauts, possessing astronomical and mathematical knowledge requiring millennia to develop. Recorded centuries apart, from vastly separated geographical regions of the planet, crumbling records of a bygone age refer to ancient astronaut Gods, mighty Olympians and semi-divine heroes who appointed human kings, taught mortals to construct weapons of war and revealed the astrological location to their home planet in the stars. Unmolested Hebrew Scriptures from the Old Testament record the ascent of several mortals to the heavens by use of divine sky borne vehicles including Enoch, great grandfather of Noah. Zechariah 6, 1-7 tells the tale of flying machines on reconnaissance missions while Ezekiel describes *"a heavenly chariot belonging to the gods*" that could "*suddenly appear over a place, hover for a time and then disappear out of sight.*" Such a "*whirlwindcraft*" lifted Elijah from earth to heaven in addition to the ruler of Tyre who was enabled by the Deity to visit the gods above in their "*fiery skyship.*"

The Bible's Genesis tale is based on Sumerian texts which describe Annunaki "*gods*" who circled the earth in their spacecraft. "*Wise lords*" who could "*descend from the heavens at will to fly through the sky*" on "*chariots of fire*", fill historical accounts from Anatolia, Cyprus and Crete as well as Sumerian, Akkadian and Babylonian records. Depicted over and over wearing "*special helmets and goggles with ear devices*" many were recorded donning curious uniforms described as "*celestial garments*" studded with odd circular objects of an unknown function. Images pertaining to "*Gods of Antiquity*" riding on finely detailed crafts that hovered high above their heads were treasured recordings of their past.

Common occurrences through the time of ancient Egypt and the Roman Empire, they continued through the Middle Ages showing up in England in 1113, 1254 and 1290, Germany in 1561 and Switzerland in 1566. Aztec, Inca, Maya, Chinese and European Renaissance era artefacts depict serpent like spacecraft streaking through the sky. Hinduism Vedas, Mesopotamian inscriptions, Greek pantheons and Egyptian hieroglyphics not to mention numerous passages from the Bible itself tell eerily similar yet slightly different representations of the same tale. Immortals: who formed a link between human destiny and a golden past when celestial beings roamed the earth.

Writers and theologians unravelling the mystery starting with the Big Bang have speculated for centuries that ancient artefacts such as the Great

Pyramids along with various stone structures and sculptures throughout the world would have to have been fashioned by advanced visitors from another world. For it is an undisputed fact primitive man did not possess the knowledge and technology required to create such wonders.

Preserved since prehistory due to lack of rainfall and not discovered by modern man until the advent of commercial aviation in the 1930s, the fantastic artwork of the Nazca Lines in Southern Peru offers no other explanation than an ancient spaceship landing site, made to be seen only from high above by celestial deities to guide their course of navigation.

A medieval tapestry housed in the Collegiale Notre Dame in Beaune, depicts the Virgin Mary against a background of what is clearly a flying saucer. Another cherished work, a painting done in the fifteenth century by Ghirlandaio again shows Mary in the foreground. In the background just to her right, there is a man looking up at a disk. The disk has large sparks coming from it and the man is shielding his eyes from the disk. A dog at the man's side is barking up at what is clearly a U.F.O. The painting is entitled Madonna and St. Giovannino and can be found in the Loeser Collection, Palazzo Vecchio, in Florence, Italy. Such important works of the time would be the equivalent to creating the most glorious artworks of today. So why would anyone stick such a curious thing in the center of a masterpiece if it wasn't there? It makes perfect sense! It was there!

THEY WERE THERE!!

Kerry T. Haggard, January, 2018

******

Chapter 1

Gringo

April 17, 1897

Catching the moon in the west, day broke as the first rays of the sun's illumination broadened in the horizon. Creeping across in the distance, lightning flared to the south as thunderheads shook in the electric sky. By day, the floor of the desert sends up waves of heat like an open kiln. By night, dust from its deadly floor is kicked up by waves of wind to sounds of yammering prairie lobos with yellow eyes. Bleached bones litter the land from the ravaging coyotes who cry throughout the night and into the dawn.

The landscape looked like a stone covered purgatorial wasteland of sun filled with sidewinders, death camas, ocotillo, prickly pear, mesquite and scrub brush among blooming artemisia and twenty feet tall aloe plants. Starry eyed lizards lay beneath rocks to hide from hungry predators. Yet in all the death, rocks and wasteland, flowers grow. A flower garden in fact, planted beneath a small town's windmill and water tower by a local judge as a tiny reminder of life and color in all this despair.

Shimmering in the dusty plain, the edge of Aurora, Texas might as well have been the edge of the world. Tumbleweeds gnashed as winds swirled and blew in the early morning, rolling and crashing into everything in their path. A large windmill turned frantically pumping an overflowing abundance of precious water out of the ground and into the town's only water supply tower. An armadillo, upset when his refuge of cemetery scrap wood topples over, scurries to find another hiding place. The sky was angry and growing clouds darkened the new day.   A storm was coming.

One that would last for 100 years.

Suffering from a smell of burnt charcoal, Aurora's west end was a burned out shell. The ravenous blaze started when a bounty hunter had discovered the whereabouts of a man with a price on his head. Holed up at the local boarding house, the ruthless tracker had decided to smoke the hombre out of his room by poking a flame filled bundle of small kindling beneath his door. In fear of the smoke quickly overtaking him, the desperado smashed through the door in a desperate attempt to escape. Now face to face, the two men fought in the hallway as the door, wall and ceiling became completely engulfed.

As flames quickly grew and began to lick the top corner of the building, clouds of angry smoke rose into the evening air. The fire continued to consume the structure with hunger as onlookers in the street stood and watched helplessly. Men held buckets which had passed from one to another in a frantic effort to contain the blaze. Some filled with sand, some with water, whatever each man could scoop up, until it became clear there was nothing to be done. Locals sat on horseback with swollen eyes watching the flames grow as the fire spread from building to building built in unison along the street. As karmic cycles spiralled, the two who had caused the inferno were burned alive still fighting in the fire. Before it was over, much of Aurora had been destroyed.

Dim kerosene lamps hung from low ceiling crosstrees in the Cantina. Over the card table the lamps emit dim rays on shadowy figures which cause the gambler's faces to appear long and gaunt like specters. Grimy and shattered in spots, outer windows complemented patched up tables occasionally used as battering rams during bar fights and friendly dustups. Wainscotted dark varnished boards were mixed with heavily worn furnishings and spittoons stationed throughout and against the walls. A sawed off ten-gauge double barrel Lefevre was propped in the corner behind the bar as well as a well worn Colt hidden underneath the back of the counter to deter hostiles from causing trouble.

Pausing from his work, the old moustached Mexican bartender, dressed in a clean white shirt and apron, looked up as the stranger entered his establishment. "Gringo." he uttered quietly in disgust. An elderly former slave with no place else to go had been sweeping the same spot on the floor for about 10 minutes. On the stranger's arrival, he gathered his broom and made haste toward the back. A bit touched in the head, he didn't like interaction with unknowns and this one especially disturbed him.

Coyote ugly with skin tough as saddle leather from spending way too much time in the sun, the dirty visitor's brown hair stuck to his head beneath a ragged hat. A muddy color stained mess, the filthy bandana around his neck at one time had been a cheerful shade of red. Making his way to the bar the stranger took off his disgusting hat placing it on the clean counter and swept clawed fingers through his oily sand filled hair. Without need for instruction, the bartender filled a clean glass sitting on the counter with whiskey.

Riding for hours, rolling clouds darker than midnight had swept through the region, covering the moon's light and making it tiresome and difficult to follow the trail. Harland Pike, 43, abruptly swooped up the shot and chugged it down. Tuckered out, the cowboy still had miles to go but this was as far as he was going to make it for a while. Motioning for another, he quaffed it down in much the same way. Spilling some on the counter in his haste, the stranger caught several dirty looks from the barman in the process. Behind a row of whiskey bottles decorating the back of the bar, the cowboy stared at his ragged reflection distorted by the poured glass mirror. Rubbing his hand across his face he grumbled, "Think I need a shave."

Not liking his looks, "Bath wouldn' hurt neither." the bartender suggested.

Shooting a hostile look in the barman's direction, the stranger remained quiet but rose to turn from the counter and observe his surroundings. The clock on the wall had just struck 6 a.m. as an all night poker game drug slowly on. One of the three lazy men in attendance had fallen asleep holding three aces and a jack in one hand. An elderly dog, his black and brown fur long and shaggy, lay asleep in the corner on the bare plank wooden floor. With so much excitement going on in this place, the stranger pulled two coins from his dusty vest. Pitching them on the counter, he turned and headed for the door.

Twelve year old Adam Edward Cochran tugged the straps of his worn overalls atop his shoulders. Wiping sleepy eyes that felt as if they were filled with sand, he stumbled out the creaking screen door at the rear of his pa's farmhouse shortly before the dawn's early light. He noticed right away that the wind was up this morning, inevitably causing the morning chores to be a bit more difficult than usual. Making his way across the yard, inside the new barn and its adjacent tool shed built in the rear, Adam finds the hoe and rake needed for his work and heads toward the garden where his father is already there and hard at it.

Saving for nearly 5 years, his pa had built them a new home in 1895 and had only the week before completed a huge barn raising to go along with it. With the help of several families throughout the community, the event had been a festive affair going on well into the night and past Adam's normal bedtime. As the young man began to tend the garden rows of freshly planted peas, peppers, pumpkins and sweet slips alongside his father, not two minutes had gone by. Strange whirling sounds in the distance, like nothing he'd ever heard in his 12 years, stopped his attention from the crops. Turning his eyes skyward, realizing the sounds are coming from above, high in the distance an oblong silver craft was creating the intense roar and headed directly toward them. 100 feet from the ground and closing fast, a trail of charcoal colored smoke drifted behind in its path. The boy's face became a picture of shock and awe. He knew no object could fly! It was a common fact.

However a shining vessel was descending from the heavens like his mother and grandmother had read to him from the Good Book. Was this the chariot of fire Ezekiel wrote of? Was Jesus at the wheel? Was God about to set down in Aurora, Texas? If so, he sure better slow down, because at this rate of descent he was going to hit the ground before too long.

Dropping to the ground in good old life saving fear, Adam looked up to see the silver craft roaring directly overhead before slowly disappearing over a ridge in the direction of town. Moments later a terrific explosion shook the ground from less than a mile away. Dropping the garden utensils to the earth, in a state between tantalized and terrified, "Oh God!" he muttered, did the Lord crash his heavenly airship? The boy ran. He had to see!

"ADAM NO!" his Pa commanded in vain. The shock of what he'd just witnessed completely dominating the child's senses, he didn't hear his father yelling, "ADAM COME BACK HERE!"

The cowboy stepped through the batwing doors and out onto the boardwalk. Facing the town's deserted street, lit by the earliest morning rays of the sun, he snugged his old hat down tight so the above normal wind gusts didn't blow it away. It wasn't much of a hat but was all he had.

During his early years on a farm in Tennessee, the dusty drifter could out run, out climb, out gun and out fight anybody that got in his way but had been tasked by his pa to tend to the well being of his defective younger brother. "*A mite touched, ain't he?*" people would say of the child.

Having to be constantly reminded to stay away from the hog pen, young Jim was left unattended by his older brother one afternoon while seeing to chores. Realizing Jim had gone silent, they frantically searched the place. Fearing the worst they checked the hog pen. The five year old had been partially eaten alive by hungry hogs, leaving little recognizable to retrieve and give a proper burial.

Since those traumatic years, Harland had wandered through ten states and four territories, had countless brushes with the grim reaper and tucked away many parts of himself. Rarely without a cold damp smoke between his lips, this broad-shouldered, barrel-chested giant had been quite a rowdy one for a time. Known for chasing fast horses and faster women, this was the first time in a coon's age he even had a horse to call his own. A horse that for some reason was becoming restless with the morning winds.

This town had a bad odor he thought while pulling out his rolling paper and cheap tobacco from the faded pocket of his vest. An acrid smell of charred wood and burnt ash. Pausing to roll a quirley with a bit of difficulty, his thoughts were distracted by his horse and two others tied to the tooth marked hitch rail. Spooked by something, they shimmied nervously from a strange whistling sound and a reflective flash of light.

Drifting through the region and finding odd work from New Mexico to the Oklahoma panhandle, he'd heard curious tales of mysterious floating airships. Stories of flying vessels, with blinking lights guided by small strange looking conductors. Harland had even seen a few unexplainable objects himself in the sky. But nothing close enough to form a fixed opinion as to what they actually were. Looking toward the south, he saw a bizarre flying craft above the desert plain surrounded by ominous clouds which hung low across the quadrant. Unlike anything the tough as square nails farm hand had ever seen or dreamed of, it was followed by a trail of smoke as it came closer and closer to the ground.

Roaring over the upset armadillo in the cemetery, the pilot of the troubled vessel feverishly attempted to navigate the winds in faint hopes of a safe landing. Weaving through the air his ship descended with an uneven gesture until hopelessly losing control. Wavering and tilting as it fell from the heavens, it clipped the outer edge of the fast moving windmill located atop a small rise and soared straight into the path of the town's water tower. Slamming into its side with a direct hit, the craft shattered with an earth shaking crash. The tower's tank exploded from the impact like a bomb, sending a wave of water, wood and spacecraft debris raining down on Judge Proctor's flower garden with bits of smoke and flame.

Then, the sound of silence.

******

Chapter 2

Tombs

100 years later

Slightly before dawn on a crisp, cool April morning in 1997. An early 1990s brown and tan west Texas official county vehicle sits at an empty crossroad in the early morning hours. The driver of the Dodge Power Wagon, Wise County game warden Denny Chote, 48, pours a cup of steaming coffee from his tall thermos. Pulling out a small pocket flask, he adds a dollop of *Wild Turkey* to his coffee. He takes a sip and grins.

Listening to one of Fort Worth's several country music stations; Denny has the radio in his truck turned down low. In this part of Texas, the game officer's job is usually a rather sleepy one, but there had been reports of poachers in the area. People occasionally hearing gunshots in the middle of the night where wildlife roams after dark. Although there were many herds needing to be thinned in the area, poaching was still illegal and as a sworn official it was his job to enforce the law. As the pleasing sounds of last year's Aaron Tippin hit *"That's As Close As I'll Get To Loving You"* flow across the airways and through the truck's speakers, Denny hears a rifle shot in the distance and frowns. Putting his coffee away, he cranks up the Power Wagon and wastes no time heading off in the direction in which the sound came.

From a spotlight mounted on an old red 1946 Dodge pickup, a beam of light scans the fence line on the side of the road from post to post.

"Keep it steady J.D." Shannon Ray whispers as he raises his gun.

"Doin' my damn best!" Johnny scolds. Johnny Dale Cochran and cousin, Shannon Ray are good ol' Texas boys. In the early morning hours of April 9th, they're out late and getting closer to trouble as the minutes pass. Looking for deer as they begin to lie down on the side of the road, 24 year old Johnny pans the light back and forth for any sign. Coming across a nice meaty one, the animal freezes as it looks into the light just as Shannon Ray, 25, lines up the sights of his rifle and pulls the trigger. A perfect discharge. The gun goes off and the animal hits the ground.

"Good shot!" John congratulates, as they walk up to view the kill.

"I could thread a needle with this thang." Shannon replies like it's no big deal. He was a crack shot and could drop a buck at 200 yards with one clean shot through the shoulders.

Blood cousins and best of friends, the two couldn't be more different in both personality and appearance. Johnny's pale hair is so bleached by the Texas sun it's the color of straw, while Shannon's is black as night and with waves most women would die for.

Hoisting the deer off the ground and throwing it over into the back of their truck, the boys head out. Their grandfather's '46 Dodge pickup is coated with seven different colors of spray can paint to keep the rust at bay. With one jury rigged vinyl covered bucket seat for the driver and a mounted five gallon bucket for the unfortunate passenger to endure, its hopped up 1950's Chrysler hemi-engine with raw galvanized exhaust gives off a distinctly loud and impressionable sound. Kicking up swirling clouds of dust as they roll along, behind them Shannon notices from in front of the steering wheel, a reflection of movement in the distant moonlight.

"Somebody comin' fast!" he worriedly warns.

The boys have set up their old truck with a row of toggle switches on the dash for just this type situation. Allowing for the truck's headlights to burn but kill the brake lights and tail lights, they make it difficult for anyone to pursue. Shannon flips the switch to disconnect the rear lamps while slamming the gas to the floor and pushing the truck to breakneck speeds. Causing a storm of dust to create a distraction behind them, they slide into a caliche side road as the vehicle pursues ever closer. Swerving from side to side around every turn, the boys make an easy trail for the game warden to follow.

Straightening out of one such turn, Johnny yells out, "Stop the truck!" Grabbing the door handle and flinging it open, he jumps from the vehicle as it comes to a sliding stop and hollers back, "Help me throw this out!"

For as long as they've been driving the old pickup they found it necessary to keep a thick heavy railroad cross-tie in the back at all times. It comes in handy to add a little weight on the rear axle for better road handling as well as using it often as a scrape to hook and drag along behind the truck to keep their driveway nice and smooth. Dumping the immense wooden timber out in the middle of the dusty road, they hop back into the pickup and tear off to a secluded area they're familiar with ahead to stop and watch the action destined to take place. Killing the trucks loud motor and craning their necks to see, the game warden's Power Wagon come barrelling around the unsuspecting curve. Denny fights to see through the thick haze of dust and darkness as the truck's front end suddenly bolts skyward with a terrific crash from the impact of an unseen object. Feverishly slamming back to the ground with a thud and a sudden stop,

"That's ol' Denny." cracks Shannon Ray. Hearing the crash and seeing the vehicle abruptly grind to a halt; the boys look on through the clouds of dust which are slowly clearing. "Damn… hope we didden' hurt him?"

"Fuck!" Johnny spits. He knows Denny would love nothing more than to have reason to kick their ass for a spell and if he realizes they're the cause of the crash, the big man will be all over them. The sound of a now warped door creaking open is heard before slamming again and an utterance of vile curses begin.

"He's alright." Shannon whispers with sweaty palms. "Come on cuz, we gotta get outta here…fast."

Momentarily the rig fires up, heading out as slowly and quietly as possible as to not give themselves away. But it's no use. Listening intently for any clue as to the culprits, standing and looking at the twisted remains of his front end and wondering how to remove the big timber lodged underneath, Denny hears a distinct sound he's heard many times before. The sound of old man Vickers' pickup with that blaring hemi motor.

A few hours later, followed by their faithful dog, Skeeter, the cousins enter the backdoor of their century old farmhouse and begin to wash their hands and arms at the huge kitchen farm sink.

"Boy that was a good un!" Shannon Ray boasts of the venison that they've just finished cleaning and putting away from the early morning activities. "Dressed out at just over 55 pounds on them fancy new scales Tombs sent over."

Drying his hands as Johnny moves to the sink and begins to wash, looking over at Shannon crossways, "Them fancy new scales ain't for weighing deer meat. They're for your 'vegetables'." John reminds.

"I know... I know..." Shannon drawls. Pouring himself some coffee and having a seat at the kitchen table, "they're for our 'vegetables'" he concedes.

Hearing a squeak from down the hall as Johnny sits to join him, they glance to see Shannon's bedroom door open. Petite, blond and cradle robbing young in appearance, Shannon's girlfriend Melinda walks out of his room totally naked but for the thin bed sheet wrapped around her.

"You're back!" she chirps with a smile. Strutting into the kitchen she casually reaches to the cabinet for coffee mug. Pouring the dark steaming drink, she leans over giving her beau a kiss on the cheek.

"Mornin' baby girl." Shannon replies with a grin and a wink to his cousin seated across the table. "We're fixin' to go into town for breakfast. Want us to bring you back somethin' from the cafe?"

"Hi Skeeter." she coos, bending over to give the dog a quick pat on the head. Exiting back down the hall and toward the bathroom, "Thanks sweetie, but I've got to get ready for school." Looking back to the staring boys, she gives them a sly grin before releasing the sheet and letting it fall away to expose her smokin' hot body before disappearing into the doorway. Shannon Ray lets loose a whistle and a wide happy grin.

John however shakes his head with an inquisitive look and questions, "School?"

"She's the math teacher." Shannon quickly dismisses, not really caring to discuss just how young his beauty actually is.

"Sure..." Johnny dismisses cynically. "I bet she's great at figures."

"Oh she is." Shannon quickly counters, "You can count on it!"

Throwing him a shitty look for staring toward the doorway, "Come on!" Johnny coaxes. "We gotta get goin'. And don't forget, you got a package at the post office we need to pick up." With a fresh look of excitement at the reminder, Shannon heads for the door. Skeeter follows.

******

Chapter 3

Bury Him

1897

Dreams are often clouded with elements of past reality mixed with visions of mumbo jumbo and nonsense. Familiar images intertwined with fantasy and interpretations, some normal, others terrifying with hints of real events, vivid memories and familiar faces slog through the sleepers' mind until waking distinguishes them from the surreal.

Sitting with his chair propped back, 53 year old Sheriff William Otto of Wise County Texas dreamed of his past. His gang on horseback with long duster coats and bandanas over eyes to hide their identity, they fired single action Colts while robbing banks and trains. Galloping alongside a passenger car from a prior moment in time, he's shaken awake and to reality by the jolt of a terrific explosion from nearby. Otto's eyes fly open and his chair slingshots backwards, dumping him to the floor. Puzzled by the noise, his first thought is it could be the town's supply of giant powder, stored in the shed by the livery stable.

"Damn what a mess that'd cause." he mumbled with a cold edge to his words. Rolling to his side on the cold floor, the pot belly stove had been dormant for hours. Rolling the possibilities in his mind as to the cause of the blast, what could have set that TNT off in the middle of the night? Surely not another fire? He wished that thought away. Aurora would not survive another blaze. There'd be nothing left.

Back on his boots and over to the double swinging glass door gun cabinet, the lawman quickly retrieved his weapon of choice, an 1895 Marlin breech-load .45. Whatever he saw fit to pull the trigger at, Otto was a sure shot but thankfully didn't have to use it much in his town. Thumbing the lever to brake the breech, he checked to make sure the damn thing was loaded and ready to go. As he swung the cabinet doors closed he was joined by Vern who was also shaken from his jail cell slumber by the unexplained explosion.

In his late 40s with dark eyes and hair, Vern was collectively known as the town drunk. Rolling off the thin horsehair stuffed cot in the open cell, crashing to the floor face first, he'd staggered to his feet with a knot building on his face and head hung low as the tiny lockup whirled around him. By the Sheriff's side, Otto glanced with some consideration to reopen the gun case and hand Vern a weapon. After a moment, he decides against it and the two head for the door.

Amid a mess of tangled bed sheets, in a room on the upper floor of the hotel located adjacent to the sheriff office, Jenni Wilkinson, who turned 30 last week, squints toward the window to see the night is just beginning to turn into day. "What happened?" she asked sheepishly.

"Splosion!" blurts out Aurora deputy Frenchie Busch as he tugs on his union suit following a wild night with his two favorite females, Jenni and Mona. The deputy had awakened to the immense blast on a lumpy worn bed between the town's only ladies of the evening. Both nearly naked in flimsy night clothes, nipples shining, pale boobs lazily hanging out and glowing like soft baby moons. Frenchie had been comfortably snoozing between the sleeping beauties till a jolt resembling the blast of a heavy Civil War cannon rocked them. Jolting Mona to fall off the side of the bed with a yelp, it was also cause for the deputy to step on her as he hopped from the wadded bedding to dress.

The ladies had their own room on the upper floor of the hotel where they had awoke with Frenchie to the eruption. The owner gave them a good rate because they were good for business. Didn't many folks come to Aurora to stay for more than a night or two and when they did most were happy to find there was some decent looking female company only a few doors down the hall. Hurrying out of the room and down the stairs to determine the cause of the explosion and make certain the hotel wasn't going to burn down, both girls buttoned what few buttons on their night clothes remained intact to cover their privates and Frenchie struggled to pull on his remaining boot.

Two doors opened within seconds of one another on the boardwalk. Otto and Vern emerging from one, Frenchie and the sirens from the other. In unison, all eyes fixated on the dusty stranger in front of the cantina across the street who stood transfixed. Wildly dishevelled from their abrupt awakening the group glared in the direction of the rough looking cowboy for clarification and confirmation as to what direction the explosion came.

Moving his eyes with a curt nod, the stranger indicated that the disturbance originated near the water tower and the small group breaks into a run toward the scene. Quietly licking his smoke, the cowboy put it to his lips. Whatever fell from the sky wasn't going anywhere so there was no need to hurry. Striking a lucifer on his trousers and lighting his cigarette, he took a drag and slowly made his way behind the others.

In the wake of the downed craft nothing of it made any sense. Arriving at the incredible scene, the stunned group stood huddled together motionless from this incomprehensible sight. The craft had partially shattered from its high velocity impact with the water tower and crashed to the ground in a cloud of smoke and steam, landing in the muddy flower bed at the foot of the tower with a grinding rumble. Silver metallic in appearance, the mysterious craft resembled a crushed metal bowl which would have measured about 12 to 14 feet long.

Casting blank looks at one another then back to the scene in confusion and disbelief, they stared at the strange wreckage, pieces of busted water pipe and splintered wooden boards that littered the area. The spilled contents from the water tower had created a small lake on the dirt landscape floor. Shining brightly like a mirror, even in the cloud filled skies of the morning and covered in mud and flowers, the majority of the airship, although rumpled, remained in one piece with only a handful of sections torn away. Broken open, the flying machine revealed one small figure inside. Slumped over. Face down. **Dead.**

Moving close and reaching his arm inside the broken vessel with caution, the sheriff pushed the pilot's limp body back revealing his face to gasps from the building crowd of, "Look at his eyes!"

"Your eyes 'ed be that big too iffin you'd seen that big ol' tower comin' towarge you!" says the drunk before being shushed by the sheriff.

"Shut up Vern! We don't know nothin' 'bout this feller, nor why his eyes is like they are."

Looking at the body, there was nothing about the small disfigured cadaver that resembled a being any on the scene had ever encountered. "*Not of this world*" as would soon be reported in local papers, his head, large in proportion to the body, resembled an upside down hard-shell gourd. His tissue structure was scaly like a lizard and its blood wasn't red but looked almost black on its small uniform. Its face had no hair or eyebrows mounted on a chinless skull with huge recessed almond shaped eyes, small slit for a mouth, tiny apertures for ears and vague nose all grouped close in a circular area on the lower part of the head. Weighing no more than a child, it had bizarre looking hands at the conclusion of thin arms which extended from a stretchy skin tight one piece metallic suit, the color and texture of the hull of the craft.

Running as fast as his small frame could all the way into town to see if his Heavenly Father has survived the impact, Adam Edward was ecstatic to meet God, dead or alive. Spotting a crowd in the direction of the windmill after catching a much needed breath, he headed in that direction.

Cowering beside the sheriff, an old Mexican woman who'd made her way to the scene makes the sign of the cross on her chest at the sight of the strange dead body. Noticing her distress, the sheriff instructs, "Valentina… lady shouldn' see this." Mona and Jenni glance at one another in their threadbare bed cloths, then back to the spectacle knowing no reference has been made concerning either of them. "Go over'n tell Roberto we're gonna need one a them cedar coffins he makes covered in pitch." Otto continued.

"Tell em to make it a small one." Frenchie adds, "this here feller ain't no bigger'n my baby sister."

"Yes Sheriff Otto!" Valentina replies, leaving the scene almost in a run.

Turning to his deputy the puzzled sheriff asks, "Frenchie, you ever seen anythin' like this before?"

"Nawww…" he replies, "But I heard stories 'bout folks seein' things like this over Texas and Okiee fer the past year'er two." Looking around at the growing crowd, he lowered his voice and continued closer to the sheriff's ear, "Say they ain't from this world, if ya know what I mean?"

"I heard 'bout somethin' like this down in Fort Worth!" a young excitable voice interjected from the crowd. One of Wanda's boys from down at the livery.

Only to be downplayed by his brother standing beside who scolds, "You ain't never been ta Fort Worth!" then harshly, "You ain't never been outside a town!"

Ignoring the bickering boys who are now cursing and threatening one another, Otto turned his attention back as a rough voice cracks from behind the crowd, "I seen em."

As all eyes turn in the direction of Harland, the cowboy and only eyewitness to the crash, "Damn things been flyin' all over these parts... an naw… they *ain't* from our world."

Thinking he may get some answers, Otto asks, "Were they from then stranger?"

The crowd now parting to allow the cowboy access, Harland took a step forward but doesn't answer. For a reply he simply points toward the skies.

With a long face Otto sighs, "Well, this en won't be doin' no more flyin', that's real and for certain!"

Not part of the on looking crowd and known as being a bit of a town troublemaker, the sheriff spots young Adam Cochran doing something he shouldn't. Picking up a piece of the metallic wreckage.

"Adam Edward! Whatcha got there?" he asks with a harsh tone. To no reply, the boy holds tightly to the silver fragment, turns and runs off in the other direction. "Dagnabbit now, you bring that here!" Otto snaps. High-tailing it between two of the abandoned burned out buildings on the west side, he disappears from sight.

Gritting his teeth with a disapproving wave, but having no time to deal with the boy, Otto turned his attention back to the crash and with a ragged voice to his right hand man, "Soon as we get this little feller here in the box, ride out and tell Sven ta bring them boys a his. Tell'em I'll pay em a dollar a piece to help move this contraption he was ridin' in." blustering as an afterthought, "and tell em to bring their mules!"

Backing away from the wreckage, the deputy recalled, "Them boys' almost big as them mules."

"That's why I want em!" Otto insists, "We gotta get this wreck over to the livery 'fore dark. Then try'n figure out what we gonna do 'bout losin' every drop a drinkin' water this town has sprayed out all over the ground!" Shaking his head to all the trouble the incident had caused and looking up at the remains of the tower dripping out their last few drops of precious water, he continued, "While you're gone I'm gonna send a telegram to the rangers." then frowning at the mess of mud and debris scattered across the area, "Judge Proctor's gonna be mad as hell bout his flower garden..."

"Sheriff…" Vern interrupts.

"Whatta you want?" Otto scolds with a ragged tone.

"Whatcha goin' do with em?" he just can't help but ask.

Adjusting his hat with another sigh, Otto turned to face the dead traveler. "Well, from our world or not... he's dead..." the sheriff reflected, "I'm gonna see to it we do the only Christian thing they is... bury him."

Drawing by Science Educator, Trevor Lewallen, Commerce GA.

******

Chapter 4

Soundgarden

1997

An enthusiastic student and eager to learn in school, twenty six year old Bonnie Reynolds was the youngest of three girls. She wanted more in life than her destitute childhood had offered and realized that to get to *Oz* you first have to first brave some obstacles on the yellow brick road.

Growing up in thrift store hand-me-downs and living in a series of rundown apartments, she inherited faded apparel only after both older sisters had worn it threadbare and couldn't fit into it anymore. During her nomadic youth, they didn't go hungry but weren't the most well fed children on their rundown Gainesville, Texas block. Visiting local food banks every month, they never went hungry but did wonder from time to time where their next meal was coming from as the weeks progressed and their few supplies dwindled. Abandoned by their father after the announcement of a third baby on the way, mom had done all she could to keep them going and the sisters formed a close knit bond not knowing what to do without the other.

At five foot four inches tall, the pretty brunette breezed through high school with perfect grades, receiving one of three academic scholarships allotted to her school. Dancing with college girlfriends to music from the B-52s, they formed their own *Deadbeat Club*, proudly wearing torn sheets in the rain after several tequila shots and a few bong hits. They weren't an overly wild group compared to most, but had fun times following finals.

As an undergraduate student of the University of North Texas, Denton, she developed a passion for reporting and took a job with their home-town newspaper to improve her journalism skills. When her six month performance review rolled around, the editor decided Bonnie's talents were being wasted and placed her in charge of a small weekly column titled, *A Century in the News*. Delighted with the opportunity for advancement, she did her best to live up to his expectations for which he had been pleased. Searching a variety of ancient newspaper articles and yellowing historical documents stored in the basements periodical files, she recapped what was making headlines 100 years before and occasionally wrote follow up stories of her own.

Until that time the column had become a colossal bore rather than an interesting look into the past.

"I want you to rev it up a bit!" her editor instructed, "give it a facelift." Since then she'd worked diligently to make interesting reading by digging and researching to find tantalizing titbits.

142 pounds of alluring femininity, Bonnie sits at her desk sipping her second cup of fully leaded morning coffee sweetened with decadent creamer. Studying her computer screen, it's filled with microfilm images from the papers' ancient archives. Raising a hand of thanks without looking up to the new mail clerk as he passes, several envelopes are placed on her desk as he moves on through the main office of the *Gainesville Daily Register*. Deep in her work, her

radio's volume turned low to the tune *Black Hole Sun* by Soundgarden, the reporter's desk is a mess of papers and notes related to her column. With deep brown eyes which seemed to sparkle with mischief, Bonnie scans through material for her next week's article. Hundreds of stories from the region concerning late 1800s farming woes, livestock prices, weather predictions and every now and then running across something she feels may be of interest in this century, as well as the last. Spotting an interesting piece from an April 19, 1897 Fort Worth daily, she pauses for a moment and begins to read…

MONDAY, APRIL 19, 1897.

A Windmill Demolishes It.

Aurora, Wise Co., Tex.,Ap ril 17.—(To The News)—About 6 o'clock this morning the early risers of Aurora were astonished at the sudden appearance of the airship which has been sailing through the country.

It was traveling due north, and much nearer the earth than ever before. Evidently some of the machinery was out of order, for it was making a speed of only ten or twelve miles an hour and gradually settling toward the earth. It sailed directly over the public square, and when it reached the north part of town collided with the tower of Judge Proctor's windmill and went to pieces with a terrific explosion, scattering debris over several acres of ground, wrecking the windmill and water tank and destroying the judge's flower garden.

The pilot of the ship is supposed to have been the only one on board, and while his remains are badly disfigured, enough of the original has been picked up to show that he was not an inhabitant of this world.

Mr. T. J. Weems, the United States signal service officer at this place and an authority on astronomy, gives it as his opinion that he was a native of the planet Mars.

Papers found on his person—evidently the record of his travels—are written in some unknown hieroglyphics, and can not be deciphered.

The ship was too badly wrecked to form any conclusion as to its construction or motive power. It was built of an unknown metal, resembling somewhat a mixture of aluminum and silver, and it must have weighed several tons.

The town is full of people to-day who are viewing the wreck and gathering specimens of the strange metal from the debris. The pilot's funeral will take place at noon to-morrow.　　　　S. E. HAYDON.

Stumbling upon the long forgotten story concerning the *"pilot of an airship"* that was *"not an inhabitant of this world"* who had *"collided with a windmill"* and then *"buried in the local cemetery"* of a town just a few miles away... now, that was something to get excited about!

"Ohhh, my gosh..." she whispers, recalling newspaper and TV reports less than a month before of *"shopping mall size"* UFOs passing slowly over the Arizona night sky in a triangular formation. Witnessed by thousands from the upper state line to the south point of Tucson, they claimed the objects emitted bright lights, moved gracefully through the air and produced no sound. The *"Phoenix Lights"* made worldwide headlines. Beside herself over the ancient article, the young reporter looks up from her computer screen with an elated expression. No *"airships"* existed back in the 1890s unless... the pilot was indeed *"from the planet Mars"* as the article suggested or at the very least... from another world.

Her headstrong editor would be overjoyed if she could do a proper follow up story on this! Taking a quick break to make photocopies of the article and reheating her coffee for the third time, she settles back at her desk to delve into the past. Searching for related articles further back before the Aurora incident, what she found was astonishing!

Years before anything powered by man soared across the airways, there were hundreds of newspaper accounts of silver flying objects that floated through clouds and left trails of smoke.

The first hot air balloons appeared in the 1700s and the Wright brothers flew their first plane in 1903, but the time period between was flooded with descriptions of hovering vessels with humanoid beings not of this Earth. Air borne vessels with various protrusions and multicolored lights were reported by thousands who signed sworn statements to the accounts throughout the southwest following the Civil War were witnessed moving through the sky from 5 to 200 miles per hour, the accounts were astonishing when you consider the fastest mode of transportation at the time was a fast moving steam locomotive which clacked along the tracks at a top speed of about 40 miles per hour.

Man made dirigibles didn't become known until the late 1800s and the most primitive airplanes were still years to come. Communication of the time was limited to telegraph, newspapers and horseback, which took days if not weeks for news to be delivered as unexplained sightings grew ever more frequent. With no defining words or references to go by since the term "*flying saucer*" didn't come into play until the 1940s, putting these accounts into words was a difficult task in the 1800s. Cowboys and farmers of the old west described these strange flying objects with more familiar names such as *bulls, bowls, dragons, serpents, cigars* and *balloons.*

According to the 1897 Farmers Almanac, between April 13th and 17th there were over 38 reported airship sightings in 23 north central Texas counties alone and in the second half of the 19th century American Old West, these types of encounters were common occurrences. These are but a few of the hundreds of documented accounts.

Fur trapper, James Lumley watched a "*Sky Rocket*" streak through the sky above the Great Falls of Upper Missouri which moments later crashed with a monstrous explosion that shook the entire forest and emitted such heat on impact that it turned the ground to glass. Reported in the September 1864 *Cincinnati Commercial*, "*the next morning Lumley was astonished to find a widespread path of destruction cut through the forest several rods wide.*" He went on to describe the "*object at the end of it divided into compartments and carved with hieroglyphics similar to those found in the writings of ancient Egypt.*"

On June 27, 1873 the *Fort Scott Monitor* reported several reliable Kansas residents scared out of their wits by what appeared to be a *"huge flying serpent, which remained in the air for quite some time."* This was also seen by several U.S. Cavalry soldiers stationed at Fort Scott, after the incident a group of farmers were *"seriously frightened"* by a serpent-like apparition which they described *"as long as a telegraph pole circling the town of Bonham, Texas, terrifying farmers and townspeople hid under their wagons and fled inside before the obstacle moved to the east and disappeared out of sight."*

The *Denison Daily News* some 70 miles north of Dallas gave the report of a sighting on Jan 25, 1878 titled, *"A Strange Phenomenon."* It told of North Texas farmer John Martin who in his words saw, *"a large saucer"* which *"grew in size rapidly as it approached"* and appeared to be *"gliding through the air at a wonderful speed."* Using the term saucer in his account of the incident, it was the first time a flying object would be referred to in such a description.

Friday, June 6, 1884 northwest of Benkelman, Nebraska, John Ellis and three fellow cowboys were gathering up cattle in a remote area when they witnessed a flying saucer crash. Reported in the *Nebraska Nugget* and Lincoln's *Daily State Journal* as *"a cylindrical air ship 50-60 ft long and 10-12 ft wide composed of a strange metal that's remaining fragments were found to be extremely light"*, the craft, *"made a terrific whirring noise before crashing to the earth and falling into a deep ravine."*

On Saturday, June 13, 1891 over the small town of Dublin, Texas a flying object exploded in the sky above the Wasson & Miller flour mill and cotton gin. The report in the *Dublin Progress* stated that *"after hovering 300 feet above with a dazzling bright light the oblong-shaped object suddenly blew up with a force so intense it was felt by nearly everyone in that portion of the city, shattering into pieces before hitting the ground."*

Strange fragments of the craft were reported to look like "*a remarkable thin substance the color of lead with strange markings of a foreign language.*"

Another mysterious flying vessel described as a "*serpent*" was reported in Indiana's *Crawfordsville Journal* on September 5, 1891. Methodist Reverend G.W. Switzer observed in the night sky, "*a creature swimming through the air like the gliding of a serpent. Swooping toward the ground then back up again, it continued over the town and out of sight.*" The same vessel was seen by two ice delivery men preparing for their nightly deliveries around 2 a.m. Frightened by the creature and skedaddling on horseback, they described it as "*18-20 feet long by about 8 feet wide, moving through the air with a great flaming eye and emitting immense wheezing sounds.*" The following evening the same object was witnessed by over 100 town onlookers and never seen again.

All this was just the beginning.

"The Great Airship Mystery of 1896-97" began in November of 1896. The first documented widespread sighting of strange silver colored airships, took place over several nights above Sacramento California where hundreds of residents witnessed the spectacle with great clarity. Reported in the November 22nd *San Francisco Call* a *"large oblong shaped craft supplied with bright electric lighting and manned crew, was moving above the ground."* People from all over California, Oregon and up into Washington witnessed *"mystic flying lights"* and *"phantom airships in the sky."* with continuous sightings throughout Arizona and into New Mexico.

East of Modesto California, also on November 22, Methodist ministers H. Copeland and John Kirby observed a *"red fireball"* with blinding lights in front and back which rose and descended before disappearing from sight.

The most startling November sighting came near Lodi, California on November 25th when Colonel H. G. Shaw, traveling in his horse drawn carriage, came upon three hairless beings. *"They had tiny ears and stood along the road while their huge cigar shaped craft hovered behind them over a lake."* When asking where they were from, Shaw was reported to have been unable to understand their *"warbling chant"* but stated *"each had a bag under their arm attached to a nozzle from which they breathed and carried something about the size of a hen's egg emitting an intense penetrating light."* After a time *"the three walked rapidly toward their ship, opened a door on the side and disappeared within."* The ship then *"went up and through the air rapidly, soon out of sight."*

Increasingly detailed newspaper accounts described sightings through December and January across California and by February mysterious luminous airships were being seen as far east as Belleville, Kansas, Quincy Illinois and communities all over Texas. According to the January 25th *Omaha Bee*, witnesses saw *"a large glaring object move at remarkable speeds then descending to 200 feet, it circled the area for a full 15 minutes before disappearing."* The same object was sighted on January 31st a few miles west of Hastings, then again on February 5th, 40 miles to the south. Sightings were reported on February 17 in the *Kearney Hub* from three men who reported a barrel sized object rising 300 feet in the air before descending and similar objects were reported in North Loup on March 13th.

Accounts continued as *The Kansas City Times* reported on March 29th an object over Topeka that *"moved parallel with the horizon with great rapidity."* On April 15 with the *Dallas Morning News* reported that an amateur astronomer gazing into the sky with powerful field glasses, spotted a cigar shaped object with a powerful searchlight over Cresson Texas that *"floated a half mile above the ground which seemed to be 50 feet long with wings protruding from each side."*

Then on April 17th came Aurora.

******

Chapter 5

Silver Dollar

1897

Francisco, the bartender in the cantina, stocked a little of everything. Gin, tequila, mezcal, brandy, sarsaparilla and of course three different grades of whiskey including a premium rye. He didn't have to keep so many varieties. Most drank the cheap stuff, but every now and again some preferred a better quality drink so it was good for business for those who could afford it. He took pride in his small cantina and wanted to have something special to offer paying customers.

Wiping his counter and waiting for news of the outburst, his thoughts were on the event and how it would directly affect business. The good people of Aurora would be thirsty and in for a drink. Not to mention gossip about what happened. Exciting things were a rare event in Aurora and the greatest majority of the time... they were bad. When the local cotton crop, a major source of area residents livelihood, was wiped out by a massive boll weevil infestation the town suffered a huge loss. A spotted fever epidemic damn near wiped out half of the remaining citizens and placed the entire town under quarantine for nearly a month. Then there was the great fire which burnt down almost the entire west end.

Rubbing a shot glass with his last clean white towel, it was time to build a fire out back and boil his aprons, bar mops and such. He'd planned the task for the morning, however with the prospect of excitement in the air… it would hafta wait. Sitting the glass down, it wasn't surprising to see Vern leading the pack as the first wave of onlookers made their way through the swinging doors. It hadn't rained in nary a month, yet piling in to his establishment with muddy boots, leaving huge brown clumps all over his just swept floor, the visibly shaken men began gathering at the bar.

"Where'd all that god-damn mud come from?" the barkeep grumbled with an agitated tone. After years of serving the same confederation he knew what they drank and poured each one's poison without delay. There was a strange silence among the population, as if they'd come from a gunfight where the party they were rootin' for had lost. Best to let them be for a while he figured, they'd start up when they were good and ready.

Vern was first to sweep up his drink, spilling some in his excitement to get it to his lips. Swallowing the fiery liquid in a single gulp he slammed the glass down and rasped, "Need'a nother!"

Puzzled, "What's all the commotion?" asked Francisco.

"Never seen nothin' like it in all ye born days!" one of the gents groaned as if it hurt to even talk about. "Feller's head swole up big as a melon and ain't got no ears!"

"What feller?" Francisco pressed, totally lost to the reference.

"One what blowed out the water tower!" grovelled Vern.

Refilling Vern's glass with rye, "Water tower?" he challenged, "Was that what all that noise was? How'd he do that?"

"Whomped it good with his shiny flyin' machine!" Vern shouted. "Looked like a giant silver nugget. Don't look like much a nothin' now. All busted up."

"Nooooo." Francisco uttered in disbelief. "Come on now, y'all talkin' nonsense. Machines can't fly?"

All in attendance nodded. "This'en did!" one added, "God save me. Saw it myself."

Looking up from the bar Francisco saw Jenni hobbling toward the cantina. Now what in the hell had done happened to her? He liked her. Not in the way a man loves a woman, although he had to admit she was a sweetheart. Her exposed curves made her easy on the eyes too. A dainty thing, she was extra clean for a whore. Took baths every day whether needed or not. Even made up a small contraption to pump salty soda water up inside her to wash out all the unwanted deposits from satisfied customers. He knew because she needed numerous pints of his soda.

She reminded him of his daughter Maggie. Who Jenni greatly resembled and had died at about the same age she was now. Thrown off her horse when spooked by an unseen prairie viper's rattle, he'd never been so sad in all his life. Couldn't eat. Couldn't sleep. Her mama fared far worse. Cried all the time, even in her sleep. Died less than a year later of a broken heart. Couldn't have been nothing else cause she wasn't sick a day in her life till all that happened. That was two months to the day before the fire. He would never forget it and now he was all alone. He knew Jenni wasn't Maggie but he could at least pretend if he wanted to and give her a bit of fatherly attention he missed so much giving to

Maggie. With visions in his head of his long past daughter, he made a wrinkled frown as now Jenni was outside dancing around in the horse trough.

"What ta hell is she doin'?" he wondered out loud. "Wanderin' round barefoot... danged if she ain't the muliest girl I ever..." With a fretful look about her, after a minute of splashing, she sat down on the edge of the trough. Messing with her foot, must'a hurt it he thought? Otherwise she wouldn' be picking at it like she was. It did look awful red. Was that blood? "Hmmm..." he mused throwing the towel over his shoulder, better go out and have a look.

"Be right back." he mumbled to none of the still shocked drinkers in particular. None commented even though a couple had turned to see what he'd been staring at outside. No one dared say nothing derogatory about Jenni around Francisco or they'd be drinking outta their own bottle outside in the dirt with the horses.

Leaning forward over the counter as far as he could, as the bartender crested the swinging doors, Vern grabbed one of the half full bottles of Francisco's best rye by the neck. Quickly retrieving it, he filled his own glass to overflowing and hastily leaned his pouch belly over again to set the bottle back where it was. Looking around, he wondered if anyone had noticed and if he might have time to get away with it again before the barkeeper came back.

Running from the hotel following the crash, Jenni had managed to slice open the inside of her left foot on a sharp piece of debris. Propping herself against the side of the mangled spacecraft, she checked her discomfort only to discover a deep gash a little over an inch in length that immediately worried her.

Still bleeding pretty good and covered in mud from tromping through the remains of the flooded flower garden, she had limped all the way back to the cantina. Spotting the horse trough filled with fairly fresh water, she'd stepped over in it to wash off her legs and feet. Inevitably going to have to pay a visit to the Doc, this wretched cut was going to require several stitches to make it right and she didn't know if Doc Sam would trade out a bit of his handiwork for a poke or not? He'd never come across to her as that kind bein' married an all, but she'd had a coin for the previous times when she needed patched up. Today she didn't have no coin of no kind and knew she'd never be able to earn any money with a crippled foot. If it got infected and had to be amputated, the last thing anyone in this town would pay for was a one-footed whore with an ugly stump and a crutch.

Jenni knew first hand about foot amputations from her younger years in Broken Arrow, Oklahoma. At an innocent time when she believed babies came in Doc McGuffey's little black bag, her aunt was unfortunate enough to step on an old board with an exposed rusty nail and gouge a nasty place on her big toe. She'd patched it up best she could, refusing to get anything else done about it till it had done turned black and commenced to spilling pus which emitted the foulest odor. Hoping for the best but waiting too long, there was nothing left to do by the time she did see the Doctor but have the damn thing sawed off. Stupid to wait so long, she remembered McGuffey saying it was "*either cut or die!*"

She thought a right smart of that foot of hers and would do whatever it took to get it healed up. Both of her feet in fact meant a lot to her, as many of her best customers often commented on how pretty her feet were even though her toes and heels weren't at all the reason they were there to visit.

"What's all this?" came a familiar voice on the verge of scolding.

"Cut my damn foot." she groaned, "We was all runnin' and I must'a stepped on somethin'."

When their eyes met, Francisco gave a slight jerk of his thumb toward the crash, cautiously asking, "Did ya see it?"

"Yeah…" Jenni answered with a haunted expression.

Saying nothing more about it, the barman turned his attention to the gash. Taking that last clean cloth from atop his shoulder, he held it out for her to take and wrap the injury. Still in the low-cut scarlet gown which clearly showed off her ample bosom, he helped her up and put his arm around her waist to help her inside the bar. "That's gonna need stitched." Francisco muttered as he helped her inside his establishment and into a chair. "You gotta get it seen about."

"I know…" the girl moaned. The type of disgusted moan a vampire may make when returning to his lair just before sunrise, only to discover his coffin gone.

"I'll send a fresh bottle with ya fer the Doc. What he don't use patchin' you up, tell him ta keep."

"Ok." she quietly thanked.

Discreetly reaching into the vest pocket hidden beneath his apron, Francisco withdrew a single silver dollar. Placing it in Jenni's hand, he said nothing. Neither did she. Slipping her cold fingers around the warm coin, she gave him a slightly embarrassed nod of appreciation and after adjusting the now crimson streaked towel tied around her foot, stood and began hobbling toward the boardwalk. "Need help?" he asked.

"Naw, reckon I'm alright." she half heartedly assured pushing out through the batwing doors.

As she disappeared from sight Francisco returned to his regular station behind the bar. Casting demanding looks to the still silent drinkers and refilling their glasses, "Now!" he began, "Tell me bout this here feller ain't got no ears!"

******

Chapter 6

Dracula

1997

Since the beginning of man's existence there have been creatures of the night. Blood crazed monsters that have dragged their bloody prints through the pages of fact and fiction. But of all the myths, legends and folktales throughout history it is without a doubt the vampire that has culminated the largest body of documentation. Published in 1897, *Dracula* by Bram Stoker remains the most definitive vampire story ever written. As for the pop culture of today's living dead blood-suckers, that gothic novel started everything!

Not a fan of horrific material in his productions, when Universal Pictures founder Carl Laemmle was first approached by his son in 1930 to produce a silver screen version of the vampire classic, less than enthusiastic about making *Dracula* he complained, *"With the great depression pushing people out into the street, why would anyone pay to watch a 48 year old man rise up out of a casket?"*

The answer to the question was staggering.

Convincing his father to move forward with the project for release, son Carl Laemmle Jr. was convinced that *Dracula* and horror pictures in general would be a good investment.   He was so right!

Not only did the film make a huge profit during a time when most movies struggled to break even, but it along with *Frankenstein*, another horror production made and released later the same year, saved the family owned studio from bankruptcy in 1931. Even with unemployment looming over one-third of the nation, citizens were standing in line to be frightened out of their wits!

Those two blockbusters of the time led Universal to produce such memorable movie monsters as, *The Mummy* in 1932, inspired by the Howard Carter 1922 discovery of Tut-Ankh-Amen's tomb in the Egyptian desert, the chemically deranged scientist Dr. Frank Griffin from the H.G. Wells novel whose experiments led him to become *The Invisible Man* in 1933 and America's first big screen tale of lycanthropy, *Werewolf of London* in 1935. Following one last theatrical release of Universal's stable of movie monsters in the 1950s, Screen Gems released 52 horror films from the Universal Library syndicated for the new great resource in cinematic history... television.

Creating a promotional package called *Shock Theatre,* suddenly hundreds of various formats were springing up from coast to coast on local TV stations with many commentators dressed like ghouls and vampires to add a little flavor to the show. Lugosi's *Dracula* along with dozens of '30s and '40s horror classics began appearing regularly on speciality programs like *The Vampira Show* and *Friday Night Frights*. The *"Children of the Night"* now frightened a whole new generation who would grow into devoted fans to keep the memory of these films alive for all time.

During his Georgia upbringing, Gainesville, Texas newspaper editor Rodney T. Grail first discovered Universal's 1931 *Dracula* when he was 6 during a Halloween marathon on just such a program broadcast out of Atlanta along with *Frankenstein meets the Wolf Man* and *The Mummy's Curse*. Mesmerized that such glorious fright films existed, he was inexplicable lured into the world of the mythical characters, the haunted settings, the sinister background music and the fiendish legends of vampires, phantoms and *"mistakes in creation"* from long ago. From the very beginning he wanted more!

Born with an insatiable desire and fuelled by a vivacious imagination from his earliest days in school this man was different. A bit of a loner, he was picked at by the so called cool kids as the fat boy who loved monsters. He'd done his best to fit in by being the mule on the playground, pushing the preppy kids around and around on the merry-go-round. Having the misgiving notion that maybe they would ease up a bit; of course it was a waste of time.

While most boys his age were thinking of signing up for pee-wee baseball, Rod was dreaming of magic carpets, flying saucers and time machines. Not invited to any birthday parties he'd really have enjoyed attending, he was only asked to a few in which he had no interest in going. Harassed by an evil 300 pound teacher named Miss Simmons, labelling him a troublemaker, she would twist his ear to make him squeal whenever the notion struck.

Coming up with a splendid solution, he simply hid in the janitor's broom closet. Skipping her class without being missed, the janitor never told, coming and going as if he weren't there. Inevitably discovered and hauled to the principal's office, Warthog Simmons had completely forgotten about the boy, having no idea that he was still supposed to be in her room.

Today Mr. Grail was editor-in-chief of the *Gainesville Daily Register.*

What had become obvious to our young reporter, as she researched further back into the newspaper's athenaeum, was that even though the term Unidentified Flying Objects wouldn't be created for another 50 years after the Aurora incident, UFOs were hovering all across the West 100 years ago and beyond.

Armed with a photocopy of the April, 1897 news article and a quick summary of her research findings, unannounced, Bonnie Reynolds marches into Grail's office without knocking. Just as he is hanging up the phone… or rather slamming it down. "Doesn't anybody know how to knock?" he roars.

Still to this day a die-hard fan and now collector of classic horror, his office walls are decorated with original movie posters from such classics as Lugosi's *Dracula, The Wolf Man* with Lon Chaney Jr. and Howard Hawks 1951 thriller *The Thing from Another World.*

Among crowded shelves on the large bookcase behind his desk, several Aurora plastic model kits sit from his childhood, a fantastic replica of the

Jupiter 2 from the 1960s TV show *Lost in Space* and hundreds of books ranging from the ancient occult to the latest extraterrestrial theories.

Crazy over his movie monsters, it was rumoured around the office that he had a long tattoo down one arm of Basil Rathbone, Boris Karloff and Bela Lugosi in an image from 1939's *Son of Frankenstein*. Down the other, *The Invisible Man* from 1933 wrapped in purple bandages. Not that anyone in the office had actually ever seen them through his long sleeve shirts and pinstripe suits, but once in a short sleeve pullover Bonnie had noticed something resembling the trailing end of a vintage doctor's stethoscope running down the side of one forearm. The wacky things men will do for the love of their big boy toys.

Not that she had any room to talk about tattoos. Bonnie had a couple of monstrous ones herself that she cherished from her college days and enjoyed showing them off every now and again, to the right person of course.

At just over 50, a bit overweight and almost bald, her editor doesn't bother to look up and see who's invaded his domain. He knows. As if speaking to the desk he grumbles, "The home office just called to deny the first vacation I've asked for in four and a half years!"

"I know the feeling." she whispers cryptically. Hopefully low enough that he wouldn't hear.

Looking up at his pretty intern, "Do you really think it's a good time for you to storm in my office?" he asks in a dry, almost malevolent tone, "What!!! Is so important?"

Back in Aurora and hungry for breakfast, Johnny and Shannon Ray are seated at the counter of the local cafe. Thin, weathered and tan as store bought leather, 94 year old Clifton Hawks is one of three old timers seated at the cafe's large front window. Taking a puff off his unfiltered Pall Mall, he pushes his sweat stained Stetson back with a toothless grin. Staring out the big window he chuckles at the sight of the game warden's Power Wagon as it limps like a man with two broken legs into the parking lot with a distinct, *ka-thunk, ka-thunk, ka-thunk*. Its tires spread wide, barely holding in place on the front spindles, the Dodge's suspension all but totally destroyed by the earlier crash. "Looks like ol' Denny's had'a little trouble." the elder yodels.

Hearing the game warden's name, the Cochran cousins pause from their plates to feel a wave of fear run through their bodies. A chill makes its way up their spine as they glance at one another but remain silent.

Standing at a towering 6 foot 4', 280 pounds with red hair that never needs to be dyed to retain its vitality, Denny's normally pale face is extremely red this morning and his blood pressure no doubt through the roof. Exiting the wrecked vehicle after spotting the cousin's crappy old truck in the corner of the parking lot, Denny wastes no time heading inside.

"Hey Denny!" the oldster warbles as Denny comes through the door, "You had some trouble?"

Ignoring the comment, he pays Clifton no mind and heads toward the two shit birds responsible for his troubles. Seated at the counter, the great man bear hugs each with one arm like a giant grizzly. Pulling them both up and off their stools he growls, "You boys wouldn' out on the mountain this mornin'…was ya?"

"Nawww!" Shannon Ray cries, "We ain't been out there in a long time!" following up his quick denial with an overly cautious, "W...why?"

"Cause there ain't no other vehicle in this country sounds anything like your grandpa's truck." Denny huffs furiously, "and I swear I's out there a chasin' it around about dawn!"

Through their discomfort and fear, the two steel a quick glance toward each other as best they can in their gripped confinement., "Now I reckon you boys wouldn' dumb enough to take that deer y'all shot over at your grandma's house…" the boys stiffen, knowing that is in fact what they did. "and I ain't got time ta go 'round ta all your kinfolk's houses and check… but I'll tell ya this…" Denny continues sucking in a much needed breath, "… next time I hear that pick up out there that early in the mornin'… somebody's gonna get their ASS SHOT OFF!!" Lowering the troublemakers back to their stools, Denny turns and walks out of the restaurant and leave the little bastards to their meal.

Old Clifton having a good old time watching the show, still seated at the red formica table, can't resist one last goad caroling "See ya Denny!" as the game warden passes. Funniest thing he's seen in awhile.

Saying nothing but smiling from ear to ear with anticipation, Bonnie proudly hands over the printout. Laying it among the cluster of files, papers and clutter on her editor's desk. "What am I supposed to do now?" he harasses, "Congratulate you?"

"Read!" she orders, knowing how to handle this blow-hard and pointing to the paper.

Flipping his glasses down with a look of sheer irritation, he begins to skim over the paper. As points begin to catch his attention, his mouth loses its scowl. His face twists and contorts, finally settling into a medium frown, "Crashed airship?" he asks looking up, "in 1897? You're pulling my leg!"

Rising from his chair and shaking the paper at the girl, "Tell me you made this up to chap me? A late April fools joke?"

"Go on!" Bonnie commands, motioning to the print out. "I found this quite by accident while researching next week's column and knew you'd go off the chain."

Quoting the ancient article with excitement, the editor huffs, "Not an inhabitant of this world... unknown hieroglyphics that cannot be deciphered." Whipping the glasses from his face, "They buried the disfigured pilot in the town cemetery!!!" Staring at his reporter blankly. "Are you for real?" he questions one final time.

"You love It." she confirms looking to the ceiling with a smirk.

Glancing back at the paper after a deep breath, "Darn right I do! Are there's any follow ups to this?"

"No idea." she replies matter of factly with a quick shake of her head. "I brought it straight in but did do some background work. There were tons of reports concerning strange activity in the skies from that time. As if the old west was filled with low flying UFOs."

"Well, if this story's true, you won't find anyone more interested in it than me!" he howls, "How is it that I've never heard of this?" Rubbing his chin, Bonnie can almost feel the wheels in motion inside his hairless skull. So far he'd held back a little in giving her choice out of town assignments, only then to have his photographer chauffeur her around. Proud of herself for impressing this tyrant yet again, with eyes glistening she stands a bit straighter as he turns and speaks. "Reynolds...what are your plans for the next couple days?"

"Whatever you say...boss."

Without even having to hear it, the look on his face told her that this was going to be an important assignment. He loved this kind of science fiction stuff and this follow up would leave a lasting impression if she could do a good job.

"I want you to go over and check it out. Aurora's only 50 miles. Ask around. Get some of those old timers talking. See what you can dig up as to his whereabouts. Some of those old folks that have been around since pioneer days are bound to know something." he continued with a hint of sarcasm waving arms and pointing, "Follow up on anything that sounds even vaguely familiar and have Porter drive you. Tell him I said to take that fancy new camera of his that I bought along and try it out."

"Yes sir!" the brunette beauty cheers with a nod.

Then just as she spins on the heels of her shoes to leave, "Oh, Reynolds!" She stops.

Fishing an overstuffed wallet from the back pocket of his seersucker pants, he produces one of several charge cards from inside. "This one's on me but bring back all the receipts and give them to Millie." he remarks handing over the card, "Now don't get the idea your going on a vacation, I want to see this story laid bare, made incisive, thought provoking!" Becoming self conscious of his coaching he dismisses with a glare, "Why am I telling you all this? You're supposed to be a professional!"

Reaching behind his desk and fumbling with the volumes of his bookcase, he adds almost as an afterthought, "And here," retrieving a pristine hardback first edition from his collection and handing it to the young intern, "take this with you. It may provide some informative reading."

Taking the book and scanning the title, *The Truth About The UFO Crash At Roswell*, published three years earlier in 1994, she shoots him a far out look and a smirk. "The truth?" she questions with a hint of mocking scepticism in her tone.

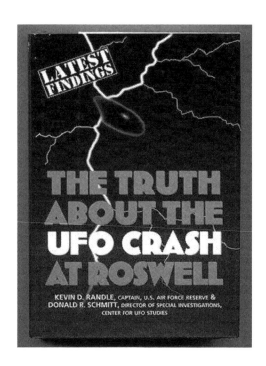

"That's what it says!" he heckles. "Or either you missed that! If your vision seems to be failing Miss Reynolds, you can pick up a pair of proofing glasses on your way out!" Anxious to get her on her way, he continues, "Now get going and go do your job!"

Saluting him as if he were commander in chief, she again spins to leave his office as she hears one last command before the door closes. With a wide eyed glare, Grail orders, **"Find Him!!!"**

******

Chapter 7

Jackpot

1897

Circling the crash, hungry overgrown buzzards big enough to make off with a small hog, swooped and stared with eagle eye perception in hopes of finding something to gnaw on. Most of the initial crowd of gawkers now gone about their business, newcomers who'd heard of the happenings in town were making their way from parts near and far to witness for themselves the scene beneath the battered water tank and have a look at the mysterious wreckage.

Regardless of Sheriff Otto's instructions, Frenchie had decided it best to remain at the scene of the tragedy. Somebody had to. Concluding his best course of action, he'd sent Jake and Tyler, the two bickering boys whose mother owned the livery, to fetch his horse, Nightmare. Boosting Mona up and into the saddle, the deputy gave her strict instructions to ride like blazes out to Sven's place, explain to him what had happened and what the sheriff needed his help doing.

He knew Sven's wife may not rightly appreciate the idea of one of the town prostitutes showing up out of the blue at their place and talking to her husband, but she would just have to get over it! These were strange times and the morning's fantastic events had made this day anything but normal, calling for drastic measures on everyone's part. Someone in official standing had to stay and tend the disaster site. Scattered wood, busted pipe and shiny pieces of the foreigner's crumpled contraption strewn about all over the ground. Then there was the wrecked fuselage of the grounded spacecraft itself partially buried in the mud beside the remains of the burst water tower. Somebody was gonna have to do some powerful digging to get it out and hauled away. The whole thing was one great big mess.

Roberto the town woodcutter and coffin maker had came out and took the deformed pilot away with the help of a couple hombres looking over the scene. Hardly believing what they were touching with their hands, they carefully lifted his small carcass from the wreck and lowered him into a child size coffin that the undertaker kept on hand in his back room just in case.

Weighing no more than a youngin' of equal size, the misshapen star man with the shiny duds looked eerily out of place in the rough cut cedar casket. Loading the box on a horse drawn cart, they carefully led the animal back to the Doc's office.

Not that that was going to help the little critter in the box much.

Gathering up all the pieces of the ship's silver shell and piling them into the smashed opening of its cockpit, Frenchie wanted it all to be in one place so they could drag the remains down to the livery like the sheriff wanted. The pieces were oddly light to be as big as some of them were and although covered with dried mud and dead flowers, they still reflected in the now bright sunlight like a mirror.

Reaching to pick up a piece of debris, the deputy felt a pang of pain in his lower extremities and wondered if it may be caused by his lumbago or from last night's strenuous exploits when he'd been the single source of entertainment for both of Aurora's most respectable girls for hire. Remembering all too well the previous evening's activities, those girls sure possessed talents few women he'd ever met did! The things those two knew and the things they could do. Years of practice he reckoned. Performances that would make you wanna slap your mama and come running back for more. The thought brought a slight smile to his face as he worked.

Some thought it scandalous for such pretty young women to behave in such a way, but he didn't see it that way. Town didn't have much trade for visitors which kept their workload to a minimum of outsiders, leaving them open for his pleasure more often than not. In return he looked out for them best he could and entertained them frequently with endless but greatly exaggerated stories of the great battle between the North and the South. Didn't matter none that he'd only been 11 years old when the war that divided the country broke out nor the fact that by the end of the conflict Frenchie had never seen a single battle. Never even had the chance to enlist for that matter.

Raised in the lower bayou country of Louisiana, he still possessed a thick cajun accent that hinted of a swamp upbringing. Several of his ancestors had indeed taken part in the battle for Texas Independence. He'd heard more old war stories from kinfolk as a teenager than he could remember. Jenni and Mona didn't know that. Not that either would have questioned any of the recollections Frenchie presented. Swallowing every word, they listened to the accounts with the greatest of interest and fascinated expressions which the deputy often thought resembled the way a good dog may stare at you if you were trying to explain something important to him.

Standing about 5 feet 8 inches in his boots with a thin and wiry build, the deputy had a tough demeanour. Along with sharp dark grey eyes, he sported a thickly kept drooping moustache which gave his face the appearance of a constant frown. The look gave him a small sense of security to help keep his actual features incognito. For there were a few things concerning his past which he desperately wanted to keep in the shadows. An ongoing effort to prevent any past endeavours from some day catching up with him.

Born a bastard child, his mother was revered throughout their parish as a Tarot Queen for her mystic wisdom and insight into reading one's fortune from the ancient cards. Covered in amulets for protection, she made a living for them selling gris-gris, charms and magical powders while performing Tarot readings which proved for many to be eerily astounding for the interpretations she saw in the deck. Once a pair of owls nested in an old hickory tree behind their house. Mama Lylou was thoroughly convinced by the depictions in the deck, that they were spiritual reincarnations of her long-dead parents, come back from the grave to watch over and protect them.

Frenchie thought the whole notion silly and kept offering to feed the birds, but mother said to leave them alone. Warning him never to leave their homeland, "energies emitting from the deck" revealed that her son would find only famine. But of course he didn't put much faith in all that mumbo jumbo.

Leaving the bayou at 20 years old to try his hand at mining, he landed a job with a mining company survey crew searching for new ore veins out of New Mexico. Frenchie didn't realize that the company's sinister plan was to take over any promising areas scattered over unclaimed pasture land by any means necessary. Should such site be inhabited by a nigger or Mexican squatters who refused to leave, company employees were ordered by management to "handle the situation." To make examples out of said rejectors as a warning to others who might be tempted to resort to similar tactics.

Driven by threats to leave their homes or face violence, several Mexican homesteaders who'd built red clay adobe cottages alongside yellow-flowering prickly pear were forced to make a stand. Three unarmed dark figures in big sombreros stubbornly showed unending defiance so mining company enforcers drew their pistols and an eruption of shots broke out killing all three of the wetbacks not to mention one of the survey crew in the process. The surveyor, "shot in the back of the head by mistake" had been secretly having ongoing relations with the wife of the man who claimed he accidentally shot him at a range of only 3 feet.

No stranger to calamity but in the wrong place at the wrong time, Frenchie was one of two members of the party who were actually doing what they'd been hired to do. Surveying, close to half a mile away, they arrived at the bloody scene long after all the shooting was over. Explaining this to executives investigating the dustup upon their return, he'd only heard the gunfire and knew nothing about what had truly gone on. But when news of the incident was somehow leaked to the county attorney and a visiting circuit court judge with a hard on for the mining company and its practices several weeks later, no one but the accused could be certain what actually had taken place. Everyone dispatched to the said location where the "murders" occurred that fateful day were discharged from their duties from the company payroll, questioned again by accusing law officers, arrested and escorted directly to jail.

Though the deceased company surveyor's death was ruled an accident, mainly because everyone seemed to like him and it was thought no one had any cause to hurt him, as for the three Mexicans, "Niggers or wetbacks, we still have to prosecute." was the attitude of the judge who explained, "not for the accidental death of the employee but for the killing of the vagrants struck down by unnecessary gunfire." The appointed defense lawyer insisted there were no grounds to pursue suspicion of murder charges due to the fact that there was positively no evidence that any crime had ever been committed.

The so-called bodies of the three chilli-pickers, "if there were ever such bodies to begin with" he insisted, had long been drug away and devoured by wild animals not to mention there was no other eyewitness testimony than the men who stood accused. Circuit Court Judge Davidson had no choice but to agree, but the local county prosecutor put up such a stink that the judge ruled to allow a jury to make the final decision and held all involved, including Frenchie, over for trial during his next visit in a month or two.

Mining was a cut-throat business at best and working under corrupt company management sometimes presented problems. Wrongly accused, Frenchie had fortunately possessed the foresight to use a different name when first registering for the job with the mining company in the hopes to get out of any such precarious situation should one ever present itself, sooner or later. As fate would have it, later became sooner when a nefarious member of the same detainee detail Frenchie was assigned to was daringly rescued by several of his owl-hoot associates. The bandits had watched the road and followed the work detail until both armed guards on horseback got close enough, then shot em both off their mounts before they ever knew what hit 'em. The detainees danced and cheered as a few of the ones who had been repeatedly beaten by the two guards took their work shovels and, regardless of the fact that the prison workers were already dead or dying, chopped and hacked their protruding beer bellied bodies to bits. As the roadside celebration ensued, the desperados regained their detained partner who quickly mounted one of the now rider less prison horses and rode off with his raiders. Leaving the rest of the group standing in the road with their bloody shovels.

Not the type of scene Mr. Busch wanted to be any part of, especially when the group wouldn't show back up to the checkpoint on time, Frenchie decided that was the perfect time to light a shuck outta there and never look back. Stealing some fresh duds two sizes too big hanging from an unmonitored

73

clothes line, he shed his striped prison wear, shaved off his beard, then disappeared as far from the area as he could go.

The only thing left behind that could have ever linked him to his wanted identity was a blurry tintype. Shot by some newspaper fella, it pictured Frenchie's full whiskered face, lined up alongside the others awaiting trial. Never telling anyone his connection with the mining fiasco who he really was or where he was from, Frenchie floated into Aurora like a ghost in the night.

He had impulsively backed the sheriff one time with a manhunt after an unfair shootout. When one of the duellers' pistols misfired, leaving the other shooter unflinched; he aimed and shot down the unfortunate man in cold blood, then ran. Frenchie had gotten hired on as Otto's number two in charge after helping track down the fugitive.

Otto had suspected more than once that his deputy suffered from a troubled past. A former train robbing outlaw himself, the two men now worked well together to try and benefit their town. They'd served Aurora together through the plague, the fire and now... this.

Gathering up pieces of the rumpled alien craft along with worthless shattered boards from the blown out tower, Frenchie piled them inside the cockpit for removal.

The stranger who'd first alerted their group to the direction of the explosion had lagged behind when the original crowd dispersed and had surprisingly decided to stick around and help clean up the mess. With a nasty quirley, damp and half smoked dangling from his lips, Harland didn't exactly seem to be the type to loiter with law officials, but after the morning's spectacular events, all bets were off and the deputy was more than grateful to have the help.

Picking up the pieces of broken water pipe, most of it had popped apart from the impact at the joints and appeared to be salvageable. The ones that were indeed broken could be cut down and made shorter. In a community as strained for resources as Aurora, Texas, every scrap of usable material was precious.

Looking around as Frenchie continued to clean up the crash sight, he grumbled, "Ain't this a damn jackpot?"

******

Chapter 8

Cinderella

1997

Instructing Porter to grab his photographic gear and meet her back at the office in an hour, our reporter left the Gainesville news office and headed home to the small apartment she shares with a college friend. Bounding in the front door to the loud radio sounds of Paula Cole's voice singing *Where Have All The Cowboys Gone?*, she finds her fiery haired roommate busily straddled atop her latest young lover.

Bonnie and the girl had met at college, becoming instant friends. Living in this spot for a little less than 5 months, their last place, a duplex, hadn't worked out so well. There'd been some "complaints" from neighbours on the other side of thin walls. "Blood curdling primal screams" they claimed to the landlord, "seeping through the thin plaster all hours of the day and night." Her mother a practicing Wiccan, Sonja possessed a vivid imagination and had no qualms about expressing her sexual passion. Adjacent residents had called police more than once, reporting sounds as if somebody was being tortured next door. "The poor woman must have been in agony. Never heard nothin' quite like it before and this ain't the first time!" More apt, the opposite tenants were jealous rather than concerned, but since Sonja was into all manor of promiscuous "entertainment" the girls figured it best to move into a single standing apartment with no one to disturb.

Bonnie had eagerly participated more than once in her bedazzling roommate's ménage a trios and was anything but shocked to walk into the scene sprawled out before her on their living room floor. Totally bare but for her hiking boots, black studded choker and fingerless leather riding gloves, the red headed vixen flashes Bonnie a wicked grin, "You're home early... wanna join in?"

With milky white freckled covered skin, smooth and clear to the point of near perfection, Sonja was covered with tiny droplets of perspiration emanating from her irresistible physique on a thick pallet placed in the middle of the living room floor. The aroma of her arousal perfumed the air. The boy beneath her on the other hand has a fearful "I'm about to get shot" look on his face due to the sudden intrusion. One he's all too familiar with. Tough life Bonnie thought. She'd only been at work for a few hours so this little session must have kicked off this morning shortly after she'd walked out the door.

When Sonja saw someone she wanted, she took them with no apologies. The auburn haired bombshell had waitressed for a while and foolishly married when she was only nineteen. Thinking she could control her demanding urges and settle down to a single man, Sonja spent three years in an unfulfilling relationship before getting out. At 25 she'd gone back to school and been having a ball ever since. Blessed with the type of feminine curves capable of filling out those little black "*fuck-me*" dresses she wore, men stopped dead in their tracks at first sight. If the notion struck, she would captivate and drain them, leaving them thirsty for more while she moved on like a predator prowling for prey.

"No time now." the reporter answers unmoved by the sight, adding with a passing wave, "I have an assignment over in Aurora..." then humorously roguing, "but don't let me interrupt."

The boy's body stiffened beneath the redhead. "Wouldn' dream of it." Sonja purrs in answer to her roommate. Looking back down at the apprehensive boy following the interruption, a kinky-haired geeky blonde who's all of 18 if he's a day, he stares helplessly up at her more than ample bosom with a mesmerized gaze. Immediately the she-devil's expression turns menacingly dark and her lips snarl back like a vampire's ready to strike, "Whadda you think you're lookin' at?" she hisses in a sultry voice, then with all her might, rears back slapping his face with a loud and painful smack. Scared shitless at this point, the teen dares say nothing in fear of another blow. Giving him a teasing wink to let him know her "love tap" was all just simply part of her game, she teases, "Naughty boy." and all is well.

Filling a multicolor knapsack with whatever Bonnie thinks she may need for a couple of days away, our columnist doesn't take time to look down at the lovers in the floor as she passes by on her way out. "I have a story to check out so it may take me a couple days..." adding with a smirk and quick peek in their direction as she leaves, "Don't do anything I wouldn't." then out the door she goes, slamming it hard.

To her great surprise, Porter is waiting to pick her up outside the apartment beside his new shiny car. A vintage 1970 Oldsmobile 4-4-2. Black with gold racing stripes and one of those fancy hoods with double air scoops, white letter tires and a wind deflector on the trunk lid. Propped on the beauties front fender, "Let's go kiddo." he quips when Bonnie catches his eye.

Opening the passenger side door and ushering her into the seat as if escorting Cinderella to the ball, "Owww, snazzy!" she cheers sliding inside.

"Might as well go in style." he replies closing the door. Itching to show off a bit, at the end of the parking lot he throws the Hurst shifter into second from a slow roll then presses his foot hard against the gas pedal causing the car to leap forward in an adrenalin causing rush. Tires squealing, the revving super engine fogs the road with a white cloud of burnt rubber.

Heading out of town a newly recorded fast moving song comes over the FM airway by singer Harvey Danger. Oddly titled, *Flagpole Sitta*, it's soon to be a huge hit. Slowing for a red light following the performance, Porter is densely unaware of the assignment he's been chosen to assist with, "So what are we doing over in Aurora?" he asks shifting the 4 speed transmission back into first gear.

"Looking for a space alien." Bonnie interjects with a wide grin.

His gaze leaving the road to snap in her direction, "Get outta here!" Shocked by the answer, he had assumed some boring broken water main or some such foolishness. Nothing newsworthy ever happened there.

"You asked!" Bonnie squealed, throwing up her hands with a shrug.

Fingers curled around the steering wheel, Porter's eyes narrowed, "What makes you think there's space aliens over in Aurora?"

"One alien." she corrects holding up a single finger.

"Okay..." he concedes, "One alien."

Flashing him a devilish grin, she proudly answers as if it were common knowledge, "I read it in the paper." Enjoying the cat and mouse banter with her co-worker, she had always gotten along well with Porter. Even though it was obvious he had a bit of a crush on her, the photographer had never been anything but professional and they'd done several small outside assignments together with admirable results. She'd always found him to be a courteous, cool dude and a bit of a goofball. Which she liked.

Porter's mother use to tell people that her son had an overactive imagination, but that wasn't totally accurate. He just appreciated cultural history and loved all things 1970's psychedelic. In his mind, if there ever was a time to live in the 20th century, it was then. A time when outrageous clothing complemented the sensational lifestyle. In particular the super cool high-performance muscle cars which at that time commanded the roads. Another aspect the man loved about that special time was the array of sensational super heroes that transported him to faraway realms of the universe, artfully created by Marvel Comics genius Stan Lee. You see Porter was and forever would be a comic book man. Big time. His collection of vintage *Dr. Strange*, *Iron Man*, *The Avengers* and *Werewolf by Night* comics were second to none for a hundred miles. For Porter hadn't grown up in The Lone Star State, he'd been raised in another land as distinctly different from Gainesville, Texas as different could be. Porter had grown up living the dream in California.

A child's wonderland of superheroes, super-villains and mythical monsters, his bedroom shelves were lined with neatly organized Aurora glow in the dark plastic model kits including *The Incredible Hulk, The Creature from the Black Lagoon, Captain America* and *Dr. Jekyll & Mr. Hyde*, all assembled and painted by him with care and devotion at his mother's kitchen table. Other shelves were stacked with volumes of Marvel Comics from *The Mighty Thor* to *The Frankenstein Monster*.

Working on the high school yearbook staff as photographer, he fell in love with snapping pictures. One thing was for sure, if he liked you and you were decent to him, it was certain your face would make the yearbook. If not, forget it! During this time, something else had become a passion for him, 1970s muscle cars. Porter felt that there was something truly stimulating about being behind the wheel of a vintage high-performance machine restored to perfect condition. It's bone crushing, tire melting superpower as if Superman himself were in the driver's seat. The gleaming look and style from psychedelic '70s high impact colors such as Hugger Orange, Grabber Blue and Plum Crazy. You didn't need a destination to take a car like that out for a ride; you simply drove it for the ambiance of the car itself.

A man of sophisticated means, when it came to choosing his own muscle machine, he wanted something with a bit of an edge. Not the typical *Spider Man* brand vehicle, but something more unique with a *Dr. Doom* look. Narrowing the search down to two vehicles, both from 1970, which would satisfy his requirements, it came down to Chrysler's Dodge Challenger R/T with the 440 magnum engine or G.M.'s Oldsmobile Cutlass 4-4-2 with its 455 rocket V8. After consideration and dedicated efforts to visit with owners of nearly a dozen of the cars in question, he ultimately decided on the 4-4-2 for its revised body style and increased performance rating which gained the reputation of "most identifiable super car in the GM house" for 1970.

As fate would have it, he'd met his boss and editor of the newspaper at a Dallas Sci-fi/comic book convention in 1989 and they had kept in touch until Grail finally convinced him to leave sunny California for the plains of Texas and go to work for him in 1994 with the promise of chief photographer for his newspaper. Since then, Texas had proven to be a good fit for Porter. He'd always resented the ever growing vampire population in Southern California who apparently believed it appropriate to suck every living human dry of every drop they could. In Gainesville there was none of that nonsense and he'd found everything he had ever wanted, a great job, nice affordable pad and his dream muscle car.

"What paper?" Porter asks in a delirium of confusion as they began to slow for a red light, "Yesterdays? I didn't see anything about invaders from outer space setting down in Aurora."

"This invader didn't set down. He crashed there and died. It's terribly sad." She really had him going now. It was great.

"When did all this happen?" he asked dismissively, "I think you're fulla shit! I'd have heard if there was anything to it." then looking over at her with a snarl, "Did boss put you up to this? He did didn't he?"

"Nope!" she snapped, "Found it..."

The sound of an angry horn blowing in protest came from behind, a peeved motorist in a green farm truck with a white hood and a yellow door, stranded behind Porter's car at the light. Several blasts insisting that the Olds get the hell out of the way, by the time Porter looked up he'd sat through the light already turning to yellow again. Popping the clutch, he speeds away with a roar and a cloud. "Dumb sombitch!" he could almost hear the irritated farmer bellow as he smelled the smoke and watched the 4-4-2 disappear out of sight.

Gathering his wits and shifting into third, "You don't really believe that.... do you?" the photographer asked chewing on his bottom lip.

Giving nothing but a shrug, Bonnie didn't quite know what to believe. What she knew was that if they could dig up something intriguing on the subject it would make a fantastic follow up story in her column which was typically dull as dishwater. Reporting on century old occurrences was terrific for geriatrics who wanted to recall what was happening when they were children, but not so much for anyone of her generation. Concluding her playful session with the big guy driving the fast car, she explained to her co-worker during the drive how she'd come across the story, what it had entailed and that she hadn't the slightest clue what they may find. What was clear was that their boss was

more than interested enough to send the pair over and check it out. As freaky as
it sounded, they were on their way to hunt for aliens!

One alien!

******

Chapter 9

Amen

1897

With the stamina to go all day, Mona Davenport had pushed the deputy's gelding to a gallop the entire way to Sven's farm. Rumping Nightmare's flanks with her naked feet in the stirrups and holding on for dear life, hoof marks churned the Earth as the animal's big legs pushed feverishly under the direction of the young seductress at the reins. Riding in as if Satan himself were closing, she galloped into the yard and reined up in front of the house where none of the Johansson clan was anywhere to be found.

Guiding the horse around to the back of the house where both barns and stables were visible, she wound up dismounting and going up to the back porch of the house where she quickly discovered the entire family sitting down inside to their morning meal.

Brought up in a two room cabin on a bank of the south end of the Brazos River near the Gulf of Mexico, a healthy looking girl now in her mid 20s, she was the living picture of her ma and possessed the brightest emerald eyes anyone in town had ever seen.

Approaching on deaf ears to the clan's huge breakfast about to get underway, its nourishment would carry each family member till supper that evening. Sven's wife was notably one of the best cooks in Wise County and one of the reasons he had married her. Quite a looker in her day and still not half bad now, Ida was extra full figured, stood nearly eye to eye with Sven at 6 feet and had been one of the most lovely women in the area at the time. Sven had courted her after a bad and battered relationship with a cowboy who'd wound up on the wrong end of a rope one faithful day. Since then she'd born him a total of seven children over the years, popping each out with ease like corks from a bottle. Five of the youngsters had been boys who'd grown into gentle giants through plenty of hard work, good farm raised food and strict Christian discipline. The youngest at 14 was already a real whopper, topping six foot three inches and weighing in at 249 pounds down at the cotton gin.

The early morning vittles prepared and laid out on the huge homemade wooden dining table was a feast fit for a king. A banquet of freshly-baked bread, complemented by fresh churned butter and thick molasses, fried bacon and baked ham complements of a former pet hog, over 2 dozen scrambled eggs, yellow grits from the mill over in nearby Greasy Bend and plenty of strong black coffee.

As Mona approached the back door of the farmhouse, the food's home cooked smell nearly lifted her off her bare feet. She'd never been inside Sven's home although she knew its location well. Deflowering not one but two of Sven's boys, she'd had rendezvous with each, more than once, on the property and knew her way around the grounds with ease.

All heads turned to the sound at the door as she stood half naked on the back porch. Mouths dropped and eyebrows raised. There wasn't one among them who didn't feel some type of stir inside. Some licked their lips; one of the boys she'd romped with several times broke into a cold sweat at the thought of the type of news she may be there to deliver. One let out a low whistle.

"Mr. Sven..." Mona called in a meek voice, pushing the hair back behind her ears.

"Mornin' young lady." he replied in his casual upbeat tone, as if she were a regular visitor despite her dishevelled appearance.

"Mr. Sven," the girl repeated almost as if she couldn't get the words out fast enough, "the sheriff needs you!"

"The sheriff needs…" the farmer remarked with a slight chuckle. Otto called on him often but never to the haste of sending a beautiful young woman still in her night dress to his door. "Come in child and share some breakfast with us."

Shocked, Mona's shoulders went up like a cat who'd suddenly spied a dog, making her boobs jiggle slightly.

Nearly swallowing her tongue, Sven's wife made a slight gurgling sound at her husband's request and spun her head to give him a disapproving look of astonishment. Turning his gaze slowly and coldly to his beloved, Sven never flinched. No member of his tribe had the right to question his decision. His stare was a stern reminder that he and only he was the head of the house and whatever he said was law.

"Oh-nooo! I..." Mona stammered, looking down at her naked feet still covered in dried mud from the judge's flooded flower garden. With multiple sets of eyes firmly focused on Mona, she realized for the first time that here she was standing before this family still wearing only the low cut sleeping gown with half the buttons missing that she'd pulled on in haste after waking from the disturbance that woke them.

"Aye! Come in dearie, I insist!" No longer a request but an authoritative command, he intended not to have to repeat his words. Opening the screen door her eyes fell to the wood plank floor as she shuffled inside heading toward the one open chair surrounding the table between the youngest of the boys who she knew only by name and one of the older ones that she knew much better.

Taking the seat and pulling it up to the table as everyone watched in silence, Sven announced, "We was about to say Grace." then giving her a slight bow asked, "Would you be good enough to lead us dear?"

Sven felt that everyone was the same in God's eyes and tried to follow that belief. Ida however was greatly perturbed, struggling to sit silent, she had seen this girl on their property before and didn't like it one bit. Although it was from afar, she watched as the dark haired hussy had made a hasty departure from a night time collaboration with one of her boys and there was no doubt it was the same girl. Breathing a contemptuous low exhale, the small gasp that escaped the wife's lips was faint but uncontrollable. She hoped that no one else had heard although the two daughters seated on each side turned to face her at that exact moment.

As the family began to join hands, as was their regular custom, Miss Davenport took the hand of the boy to the right and the one to the left, their rough work hands wrapping gently around her smooth slim fingers. The action caused both boys to tingle like a bee hive and their lower extremities to swell almost as hard as the barrels of their Smith & Wesson revolvers. There was a sly exchange of smiles from her and the handsome blond headed boy seated directly across the table who she'd been with a few times. Regardless of never uttering a prayer in her life, Mona knew that Mr. Sven, as she called him, was not a man to make excuses to so she plundered forward.

Short and sweet the guest bowed and mumbled, "Thank you Lord for this food an' this family…amen."

A contemptuous "amen" echoed slightly from most but not quite all seated. Certainly not from the wife who was in pure astonishment that such happenings were taking place at the dining table. Ida's face was now flush to a point where she couldn't have spoken even if she wanted to.

Amused to no end by all this, Sven chuckled and smiled a satisfactory grin. He knew the girl. Knew exactly who she was and the professional activities she did to sustain herself. "Thank you dearie." he announced with almost a whisper, then motioned for her to be the first to take from the food. To him she was a guest at his table, nothing more nothing less. He knew her to be a kind and decent person with a fine friendly personality and her occupation concerned him none.

Looking out at the feast laid before her, a pang in her stomach reminded Mona that she hadn't eaten a decent meal in days, maybe weeks. Certainly not to the extent of all this. Hesitating no more, she reached first for the platter of delicious looking scrambled eggs before passing it over to her right and quickly reaching for another. With a curious dumbfounded stare at the unprecedented spectacle playing out before them, although Sven's wife had totally lost her appetite, the others watched in near silence as the visitor heaped her plate with hefty portions akin to the size the boys would have taken for themselves. The only thing more delicious looking than the food at the table was Mona.

"Now!" the tribe leader bellowed from the head of the table, very pleased with his actions and their results, "What service does sheriff William require of me this fine mornin' aye?"

Stuffing her mouth and shaking her head to the recollection of the morning's events, "Don't even know how'ta explain it," the girl began, "This oblong silver boat with a little scaly man inside fell right outta the sky."

"Outta the sky?" one boy erupted.

"Quiet!" Sven cautioned.

Following a moment of awkward silence, "The vessel he was commandin' landed atop the big water tank and busted it all ta pieces." she injected through the spoonfuls of food.

Dazzled eyes from his family turned toward Sven for any comment on such a fantastic story but he exhibited no emotion, simply prompting the girl, "Go on..."

Taking a moment to breathe between bites, Mona continued, "Well, Frenchie sent me ta tell ya sheriff needs you'n the boys to help move what's left over to the livery." Opening her eyes wide and stretching the muscles in her face the girl demonstrated with her actions, "It's a great big shiny thing and Otto said tell y'all he'd pay a dollar a piece…"

"A dollar a piece!" blurted the 15 year old uncontrollably.

Sven narrowed his eyes to yet another outburst at his table but refrained from scolding the boy. "Sorry pa…" the child muttered.

"No need." Sven dismissed with a slight shake of his head. This he understood was very exciting to the lad. Probably the most excitement he'd seen since the fire that wiped out half the town. Turning his gaze back to the still eating girl, he mused cautiously, "I see…" thinking further about the situation for a moment, he smiled a tad and nodded, "Eat up boys! We gots work to do!"

Swallowing down the last bite of food that her petite frame could possibly hold, Mona remembered one last important thing, "Oh!… and he said ta bring your mules!"

******

Chapter 10

Rats

1997

Midway between Aurora and Rhome, Denny Chote stands in front of his busted up patrol truck watching a greasy, round faced mechanic struggle to shimmy his chubby self out from underneath the truck's mangled front end. A burly bearded individual in his mid forties with a good size pouch hanging over his belt, "Denny?" Frank asks of the vehicle's damage with a quizzical look as he staggers to his feet and scratches his nose, "How the hell'd you do all that?"

"Hit a railroad tie." Denny admits in disgust.

"Railroad tie! Damn! Couldn' you see that big sumbitch settin' in the middle'a the road?"

Frustrated beyond words, Denny holds his tongue saying nothing.

Long overdue for a facelift, Frank's Auto Repair was a ramshackle garage, haphazardly thrown together from whatever scrap materials were lying around at the time of its construction. A dilapidated structure appearing on the verge of collapse, it was actually quite sound for its old age. The front of the building was covered in heavily weathered sheet metal, nailed to its sides to keep the wind and cold from seeping through the gaping cracks. An uneven rusty tin roof covers the top of the establishment and it's impossible not to notice the collection of homemade *BEWARE OF DOG* signs, some old, some new, nailed prominently in various places. One extremely large *BLOW HORN FOR SERVICE* sign was mounted atop the building's front roll-up door.

Unbeknownst to Denny and Frank inside, a new employee of the local used car lot, a young punk cowboy dressed in fancy jeans and long hair who thinks he knows it all, pulls up outside in an ageing Ford van to make a delivery. Having never been there before he pauses to glance toward the side of the shop where a long dead Cadillac DeVille sits. A flop-eared goat stands carelessly upon its trunk lid eating the vinyl top off the car. Looking back at the array of immature postings, he sees not a vicious canine around the yard, only an innocent enough orange and red shaded Pomeranian. Sitting calmly on his small bed in the corner of the overhang hooked to the end of a long thin rope, the small dog appears innocuous enough. Convinced that this couldn't possibly be the "vicious canine" in question, he exits the Ford with disregard to the warnings and, in his hard rock t-shirt, heads toward the door.

All good and according to plan as he walks, calmly and quietly waiting for the perfect moment, the fluffy devil dog strikes with all its terrible fury. Dropping and shattering the delivery, running for his life back to the safety of the van, the now enraged animal follows viciously biting the flesh on his legs.

Attempting to flee the bloodthirsty killer, the young know-it-all snatches the driver's door open and flings himself inside. Followed by the innocent dog just as the door slams, the beast is now trapped inside with him. Clawing and crawling his way from one bucket seat to the other like a madman, he fumbles for the passenger side door handle, the hound from hell snarling and biting for all its worth. Crashing to the gravel covered ground as the door swings open, the naive fool slams the door shut with the mechanic's pet still inside.

Interrupting the conversation inside, Denny and the mechanic hear the commotion out front. Squinting his eyes, "Oh shit! Not another one?" the round face fellow growls. Opening the door they see the boy standing with a dumbfounded expression, blood seeping into his sneakers from a dozen wounds on naked ankles. "Jesus creeping God boy! What the fuck'r you doin?" Frank bellows, "CAN-YOU-NOT-READ?"

Denny bows his head to try and keep from laughing. Under the circumstances, it's hard as the enraged shopkeeper continues, "Stupid sumbitch! You're the third fuckin' asshole this year too damn smart ta read my signs!! Whadda ya think I nailed em up there fer?"

Just in the nick of time before Denny doubles over in laughter Andrew Shift, the current sheriff of Wise County, pulls his patrol car in front of the shop to give Denny a lift. Phoning his friend of the morning's incident, the sheriff had offered Denny a ride into town and was there to make good on his promise.

"Gotta go Frank," Denny flairs, "call me when it's ready." and heads for the car. As the two officials drive away, the bleeding young man and the mechanic stand side by side looking back into the windshield of the van. Glaring back, the angry dog, fangs bared, is ready for the next round.

Spotting the town cemetery as they reach the outskirts of Aurora, Bonnie and Porter pull in the entrance thinking that with a little luck they may be able to solve this mystery in no time. Flipping her sunglasses down to shade her eyes as she exits the shiny Oldsmobile, they split into different directions and begin searching the area for any turn of the century headstones. Wandering from marker to marker for nearly a half hour and finding none dating before 1911, Porter arrives back at her side offering, "Nothing before 1914 that I can find." The interim reporter catches sight of an older man with a shrub trimmer and starts in his direction for guidance.

"Excuse me…" she asks with a tip of her shades and in her sweetest voice, "are you the caretaker?"

"Here, the courthouse, sheriff's office, the park." the man rattles offering out a polite hand, "Yes ma'am, whether it's plantin' flowers or diggin' graves… I'm your man."

Thinking this is the fellow to help her; the reporter gives her best handshake. "Oh, good! I'm a columnist for the *Gainesville Daily Register* and we're searching for graves dating back to the late 1890s. One in particular for a follow up story I'm working on. Would you possibly know where those are located?"

"No ma'am." he answers despairingly, "Me'n my boy moved here 'bout 6 years ago. Got no idea of anything before that."

"Rats!" the reporter frowns while biting her lip. Maybe this won't be as easily as she first supposed. Looking over to Porter, she wrinkles her face and says, "Must be another graveyard somewhere else." then after feeling a pang of hunger in her stomach, back to the man asking, "Well then, can you recommend a good place for lunch?"

Pointing the pair in the direction of the town cafe, 43 year old Clarence Maney watches as the two journalists climb back in their black beauty and drive toward the downtown area. Clarence did know of the grave she was speaking of. There was only one burial place in Wise County any news reporter would possibly be interested in from that far back. He and a very small select group had been successful so far in keeping it a secret but something gave him the uneasy feeling it may not be so easy to keep under wraps this time. That look of determination in her eye and in her voice worried him some.

In the official Aurora city employee files, Clarence was one of the few actually on the town's payroll. Listed as groundskeeper, he was in charge of maintaining just about every city owned property inside the city limits. Now the second week of April, the weather was clear and there was grass to be mowed and hedges to be trimmed. As the seasons changed so did his list of duties from landscaping in the spring, to summer clean-up, then preventive winter maintenance. The mayor's assistant had approved for Clarence to have a part time helper since his responsibilities were so distributed, but Clarence would rather do what was needed at his own pace and to his own liking.

He'd moved to North Texas with his young son Jo following a failed marriage. Feverishly independent from their first date, it didn't take long for Clarence to become totally infatuated with Tonya. Her mom, a true Arkansas hillbilly, thought he was the greatest thing since processed cheese and was genuinely happy that her wild ass daughter had found someone decent to go with. Renting a single wide trailer and moving in together, as in most cases with young stupid love, things went smoothly for a short time and Tonya wound up pregnant within the first six months.

Intoxicating delusions of grandeur were short lived however, for after the arrival of baby Jo, Tonya began spending all her time with a rail thin hobgoblin named Tammy who she had met at work.

 Quickly becoming "best friends" the two were soon wearing wild matching outfits and riding the roads around Clarksville all hours of the day and night. Drinking heavily, taking pills and coming home wasted, things went to hell pretty quickly from there.

Not showing up at all one night, Clarence went out looking, only to find her lying crossways on the asphalt of a lone country road covered in mud. Running off the slick road while going too fast, one tire blown from the rim, one window blown out, the mother of his beloved child was lying on the side of the road, thrown from the wreck.

"Goddammit Clarence!" police officer Bobby Evans, summoned to the emergency room by hospital employees, berated, "This is what happens when you bed down with dogs! You get up covered in fleas! Now get rid'a that sleazy whore and get yourself together!"

Not one to sugar-coat the truth, this was the kind of cop who would hunt you down and lock you up in an instant if he had a mind to. The officer particularly despised the crowd his girlfriend had decided to run with, "What you do or don't do don't make a damn to me," he told Clarence, "we all fuck up now and again, but learn from your mistakes! Best thing you can do for yourself and that boy is to get as far away from that trash as you can."

The message stuck and when his uncle Clifton from Texas learned what was going on, he suggested to bring Jo, move to Aurora and live with him in his big old farm house for a fresh start. Uncle could possibly even get him on as a city employee. Applying for sole custody and getting it with no trouble, he decided to pull up stakes. Packing what few things they owned, father and young son were headed west before the end of the week and had never looked back.

Kuff's Koffee Kup was the only cafe in Aurora and one of the few local landmarks that hadn't changed much since the '50s. It's store bought window sign, proudly advertising "*AIR CONDITIONED*", still hangs in the same spot as it has for over 30 years right above a faded hand drawn one that claims, *"Our coffee is damned delicious!!"*

Wandering inside the front door, an attached cowbell alerts the room as Bonnie breathes a sigh and Porter takes a seat at the counter. Sitting on the very stools Denny had lifted the boys off of only a short time earlier; the atmosphere is filled with the smells of fresh coffee and sizzling meats. "Number 3." Porter orders, "Extra cheese. Extra pickle."

Looking at the small billboard menu mounted on the back wall above the counter, "I'll have a B.L.T. and a Diet Coke" Bonnie says politely. Then quickly asking the waitress, "Do you happen to know if the town has a local historian?"

Clueless and unconcerned, "Ah what?" the hostess drawls.

"A person who may know some details concerning the town's past."

"Nawww…" the waitress frowns, "but you can ask them." she continues, pointing to the three ancient looking gents seated beside the front window. All of whom are daily fixtures in the cafe. "Old croaks", she tells with a snarl, "all they ever do is holler for coffee and thump ashes on my damn floor," then raising her tone just enough where they're sure to hear her, "and don't none of 'em know how'ta tip!!" Rocking slightly back and forth in their chairs with big grins of satisfaction, the three nod in agreement.

Never shy, Bonnie slips off her stool, removes the xeroxed article from her bag and heads to join the "croaks" at their table. "Hello boys!" she hoots. "I'm Bonnie Reynolds from the paper over in Gainesville. Maybe you can help me with a follow up story I'm doing on an event that happened here a century ago." Sliding the print out across the table for them to look at, all three lean forward. None of which can read anything without powerful eyewear, of which none have it on them.

After a long moment of staring, one cries, "What's it say?"

Never missing a beat, the young woman smiles at the humour of the situation and begins, "It talks about a spacecraft that crashed into a windmill and indicates that the pilot was killed and buried somewhere here in town." adding sharply, "I'm trying to find out where."

The oldest of the three, Clifton, the same old codger that was ragging Denny earlier about his truck, remains quiet and still. "I've heard a couple different stories," the youngest of the three, Horace, speaks up, "but I didn't get here till after the war in '47."

Chiming in, Albert, the third man excitedly contributes, "I heard it was a little bitty feller in one a them hot air balloons got blowed off course from the sideshow down in Mexico. Reason he's so small was cause he's a midget!"

Pursing her lips into a sideways frown of frustration, Bonnie watches as Horace and Albert cackle and coo over the unfunny reference to the popular *wizard* story. Seemingly un-amused, Clifton gets up from his chair abruptly and in a low tone that was anything but soft grumbles, "Sounds like fairy tales ta me!"

Sensing a strange vibe to the ancient man's sudden anger, the reporter turns and watches him hobble across the cafe floor toward the door. Her intuition screams that that old fart knows more than he's telling. But what?

******

Chapter 11

Confederate

1897

"Jenni darlin'... you gotta be more careful." said Aurora's one and only doctor, an older smooth-shaven gentleman with spotlessly boiled white shirt, greying hair and blue eyes. Doc Sam always wore a black bolo tie with cravat held in place by a stick pin and a frock coat summer and winter. Earning his medical degree shortly before the conflict between the North and South broke out, he'd enlisted for the Confederacy and done his part to save as many souls on each side as humanly possible. Before scrubbing his hands with a cake of homemade lye soap, he filled a large bowl with fresh water from his pump handle sink and carefully snugged his work spectacles into place. "This is the second time I've had ta stitch you in as many months."

"Third." Jenni quietly reminded holding up three fingers and pointing to her right palm which had got cut on a broken bottle following a late night bar brawl last October.

"Oh yeah…" Doc said pursing his lips, "Forgot about that one."

She had knocked lightly then without waiting for the Doc's response strewed inside his office, head down, not even bothering with a good morning. Waiting anxiously, her curiosity got the best of her as she timidly asked, "Is the little man here?" Quickly looking down in a mix of sorrow and confusion.

The Doc's eyes widened and he nodded his head in a quick motion, "He's here alright. Brought him in little while ago."

"What is he?"

"I don't rightly know..." Doc replied with very little expression, "But I can tell ya one thing," he rasped looking into Jenni's eyes, "He-ain't-human."

"Ain't... human?" she covered her mouth with a slight gasp.

"Ain't from this world. Don't rightly know which one he's from," he jabbered, "but it ain't ours. Said they found some strange documents on him but nobody can decipher their meanin'. Wrote in symbols. Looks like gibberish but I reckon he could read em." Nodding to his patient, he asked, "Did you see'em?"

Jenni nodded, with no words to say. Still in shock of understanding that the mysterious traveler was actually from another planet somewhere out in space.

"Need I say more?" he intimated as they exchanged glances.

"Reckon you did your best for him?"

"Done all I could. Packed him in one a Roberto's boxes. Nothin' else to be done. Was dead when he hit the ground." then shaking his head in confusion, "Somethin' needs done quick though, I just got done examinin' him and he's deterioratin' fast. Tissue structure from wherever he's from obviously don't agree with our air. But enough of that." he insisted, "Let's get you fixed up."

Happily married and devoted to his wife Katie and son Darrell, Doc Sam did double duty as town undertaker as well as chief physician and sometimes filing in as mayor. A surgeon in the Civil War, he'd seen more than his fair share of both caring for the living and the dead during those horrible times. When Texas declared its secession from the United States in February 1861, it joined the Confederate States on March 2nd with the Texas Declaration of Independence and the replacement of Sam Houston as governor when he refused to recite the oath of allegiance to the Confederacy.

Over 70,000 proud Texicans were recruited to serve in the Confederate Army versus a mere two thousand to Union Forces who "*musta had kinfolk up north.*"

In 1862, Doctor Richard Samuel Malcolm received a commission as assistant surgeon and was on site for such skirmishes as the Second Battle of Sabine Pass in 1863. Serving with Company F of the First Texas Heavy Artillery Regiment, he treated wounded soldiers from both sides as his unit turned back a much larger invading Union force from New Orleans to occupy Texas. History would eventually look upon the battle as the greatest victory in history prevailing against overwhelming odds.

Regardless that anaesthesia was discovered in 1846; it was in such short supply during the Civil War that it was as if it didn't exist. When available, ether or chloroform, or a mixture of the two, was such a deadly cocktail to administer on the battlefield, often the patient simply never woke up. In many cases it was a blessing. Performing only the most necessary amputations with crude medicines and shortages of medical supplies under battlefield hospital tents, Doc Sam, as he began to be called, would work for days and nights to the point of exhaustion. Wounds received at the Battle of Galveston, then held untreated for a time by Union forces, made the Doc's leg and hip hurt daily. The pain became a constant reminder that he survived when so many others had not. News of the surrender of Lee at Appomattox finally reached Texas in April 1865 and it was met with mixed opinions among troops whether to stop fighting or press on for the good of the former republic. Officially surrendering on June 2nd, Texas was now able to begin its reconstruction.

Following such tumultuous times, Doc Sam returned to Dallas, set up a local practice and became a respected member of the community. Ready for change some years later, he met the love of his life, Katie Ann and followed her home to Aurora. Selling his Dallas office and opening up for business in the small town just north of Fort Worth, he instantly became local physician, coroner and undertaker all in one. As country doctor he treated the residents for a wide range of medical ailments such as broken bones, chronic conditions and acute sickness. Although vaccines had been developed to prevent cholera, anthrax and rabies, Doc's shelves were still lined with such eerie elixirs as Sagwa - a blood, liver and stomach renovator, Slippery Elm - to soothe inflammation of the bowels and urinary tract, Mug-wump - for the prevention of venereal disease and Swamp Root - for the kidneys. Administering a variety of treatments such as opium to counter diarrhea, willow bark to reduce fever and camphor to make a wound poultice for preventing infection, he doctored the local folk to the best of his ability.

Watching the swinging pendulum movement of the clock on the wall in an effort to distract herself, "Can't ya just bandage it up?" pleaded Jenni.

"Split too wide!" Sam replied lifting the oil lamp from his desk and placing it alongside the injured foot. "Gotta stitch it."

A groan of irritation purses the girl's lips in bitter anticipation of the stinging pain to come. Two years prior, a cyclone had whipped through town and ripped the roof off several buildings. Wandering too close to a stray sheet of tin roofing, a sharp corner caught her calf, slicing it open like a razor for the grand total of 13 painful stitches. Hurt like sin for weeks.

Digging through his medical cabinet in search of a hoop needle and surgical thread, "Take a couple swigs off that there bottle you brought." Sam recommended.

"I'll manage." Jenni whined with a frown.

"No!" he prompted, "It'll help more'n you think. You gotta hold still or it's gonna make it worse on us both."

"I'm a beer girl," she retorted, "that stuff makes me sick ta my stomach. Sure could use some coffee though?"

Looking across the room to the cold pot belly stove "Ain't got no coff…" Doc began just as the front door burst open and in stepped Dallas newspaper ink slinger, S.E. Hayden.

"WHERE'S IT AT?" the man yelled with a wild eyed expression.

"Mornin' to you too S.E." the doc calmly replied with a slight tone of annoyance, "If you're gonna stay, shut the door and go have a seat in that chair over by the stove."

"Talk is he's from Mars!" the Aurora cotton buyer/part time newspaper writer for *The Dallas Morning News* exasperated as he closed the front door.

"Nobody knows where that fellers from no more'n I do." Doc said begrudgingly as the conversation was distracting him from his work. "Ain't too sure about Mars, but he's from somewheres out there." he continued rolling his eyes toward the ceiling.

Thinking he might like to argue with Sam, "But T.J. Weems said he…"

"T.J. Weems don't know his ass from a hole in the ground!" Doc demanded, "Now… either you sit down… and keep quiet... or you gotta go!"

Taking a look around, Hayden does as told without further annoyance and meanders over to the cold stove and into the rickety rocking chair. Creaking badly as his weight relaxes, Hayden wipes the sweat from his head with a pocket rag. Running to Doc's office to see if the rumours were true and if so view the creature for a report to the paper, "Can I see em?" he asked meekly.

"You can." Sam continued with a slightly sharp note, "But NOT till I'm done here with my patient."

Sitting on the Doc's work table with her back propped against the wall and leg stretched out to the corners edge, Jenni was agitated at herself for not paying more attention to where she was running earlier.

"This is gonna sting a mite." he warned, dousing a little alcohol over the wound and wiping it with a clean cloth.

"Sheesh!" Jenni hisses through clenched teeth as the burning inevitably makes her leg jerk and twitch. "You ain't usin' the whiskey?" she asks, struggling for something to say to keep her mind occupied and away from the pain.

"That's fer drinkin'." he announced, removing the cork and taking a slug of the fiery liquid. Setting the bottle down and picking up the bright purple medical bottle directly beside, "This here's antiseptic. Made for cleanin' wounds." he continued in a bit more gravelly voice from the effect of the strong liquor.

"Could I..." Hayden interrupts yet again with a tone of desperation as Sam and the girl casts looks his way, "...have a swig of that Doc?"

"One..." Sam insists with a nod as Hayden lunges for the bottle, "If you'll sit there and be quiet till I'm finished!"

Closing the freshly cleaned cut together with two fingers and inspecting how to proceed, "What'd you step on hun?" the Doc asks apologetically.

"Damn if I know," Jenni answered wrinkling her nose. "We'ze all runnin' just before light to see what shook us outta bed. Diddn' know I'd even cut it till I felt it stingin'." Holding up her hands she concluded, "Looked down and it was bleedin' like a pig hooked on a barbed wire fence."

"Ain't too bad." Sam comforted dipping the needle in antiseptic. "Four or five stitches should close it right up." Taking one last drink from Francisco's bottle before digging in, he supped in a breath, "Ready?"

******

Chapter 12

DeLuxe

1997

Hungry for lunch and ready to put the mornings rough beginnings out of his mind, Denny and his pal the sheriff pull in front of Kuff's just in time to see old Clifton stagger outside and slam the door. Looking flustered and marching off down the sidewalk in a huff, the men in the patrol car glance at one another suspiciously as to why the elder may be leaving the cafe so early when he rarely goes any place else.

"Wonder where Cliffs off to this early?" Denny asks.

Making light of it, the sheriff comments, "Hell, I diddn' know the ol' buzzard could still move that fast." The two look at one another and grin.

Cautious about her figure and equally picky about her food, Bonnie nibbles at her sandwich inside. Her thoughts are distracted as she turns to watch her overweight cameraman devour his double greasy burger and side of fried fries. "How can you eat that?" she asks.

"Slowly." he grins, offering, "Wanna bite?"

Not to even dignify the question with an answer, she turns in the other direction just as the two officers enter. Uninterested in her meal and praying that someone with an ounce of intelligence has at last came her way; her eyes brighten as she bounds from the stool to greet them.

"Excuse me Deputy…" she begins abruptly at Denny stopping the two tall men cold.

Chote lets out a hearty chuckle at her mistake as the real sheriff corrects with a polite, "I'm sheriff Shift ma'am."

"Ohh, I…" she pulls her wrist to her mouth and begins to apologise.

"It's alright darlin'," Denny interrupts almost laughing out loud, "most everybody makes the same mistake." as he notices the embarrassed expression on the young lady's face.

Although not a small man at 5'10", 175 pounds, standing beside Denny's hulking physique, almost anyone could confuse who was second in command. Removing his amber colored sun shades, now a touch annoyed, Shift huffs to his friend, "Why don't you find us somewheres ta sit before your ass is walkin' home?" then turning his attention to the lady, "Pardon him Miss, sometimes he thinks himself a comedian. How can I help you?"

Flashing the photocopied article a bit closer to the law man's face than he would have liked, the reporter begins, "I'm trying to do a follow up piece on this. But no one around here seems willing to help me."

Uhh ohh, trouble's come to town yet again, the sheriff thinks silently. He's seen this particular newspaper clip more times than he cares to remember and knows not only what she's referring to, but a lot more. Remaining calm, but at the same time overly cautious to his response, he asks, "I'm sorry… Who'd you say you worked for again?"

Norman Rockwell called him *"The Boy Who Put The World On Wheels."* After founding the Ford Motor Company in nineteen hundred and three, Henry Ford was the first U.S. automaker to perfect the moving assembly line in 1913, greatly improving not only production speed but quality control. Born in 1908, the car that put the world on wheels, the Ford Model T slowly evolved until 1927, phased out only then by insistence of Henry's son Edsel and company executives who demanded an all new car was long overdue.

The first of its kind with all 8 cylinders inside a single casting, Ford introduced a revolutionary new V-8 engine in 1932. Its simple design and astonishing speed, combined with all new art deco styling and elegant, front opening "suicide" doors introduced in 1933, made the '34 Ford V-8 the fastest and most reliable car in the low price field. Greatly improving year by year, by the close of the decade the Ford V-8 had adopted among other things the more reliable system of hydraulic brakes. The cars last year for screw in bulb headlights, roll out windshield frame for ventilation and floor mounted three speed transmission shifter was 1939.

On an old metal bucket in the middle of their grandpa's barn, Johnny Dale sits, hard at work on his prize project; reassembling a vintage panhead Harley-Davidson motorcycle, now mounted on a shiny new assembly stand. Accompanied by Skeeter, the boys faithful Catahoula herding dog, with one blue eye and one brown eye, his coat is silver grey and covered with dark splotches and rusty feet.

Back in a far corner of the barn sits a dust covered 1939 Ford DeLuxe Coupe. Bought by Johnny's grandpa back in 1960 from a former Wise County bootlegger, the Cloud Mist Grey classic was used as an everyday driver for years before being handed over to John's father as a high school graduation present. Not seeing the road since Johnny's dad left for the Army and never made it back, it now waits patiently for a full restoration alongside an ever growing mound of new old stock Ford parts to aid in the project.

Built shortly before World War II, Johnny's dad always remarked what a special time in history that car represented. Although a vague memory, Johnny could still remember riding in the car when he was very young and how it was like cruising in a time machine. As soon as the Harley was finished he was going to begin with it and he couldn't wait!

The 1950s panhead also had belonged to his dad. John had been planning the bikes return to glory since he was 15 years old and was now ecstatic to see it in its final stages of completion. Tightening down the bolts holding its handlebars in place, he hears Shannon Ray call out, "Looky what I got back." Taking a carefully wrapped item out of the box retrieved from the post office earlier during their morning run to town, the cousin walks over unwrapping the fuel tank for his own bike. "Wow!" he boasts of the item recently sent off to be repainted.

"What the hell is that?" Johnny snaps.

Smile now fallen away, "My gas tank." he answers in confusion, "What's it look like?"

"Looks like the ass end of a zebra!" Johnny scolds, "Who da you think you are? Ted Nugent."

His face now a picture of grief, "I seen it in a movie with Joe Namath." Shannon cries, "He rode a chopper like the one I'm buildin' in *C.C. & Company*." Holding the black and white stripe fuel tank out as if to inspect, he adds, "I had mine painted ta match."

"I shoulda known." Johnny dismisses, going back to work on the bike, muttering "Whaddya expect from a guy that plays football wearin' panty hose?"

"Awww, come on now…" Shannon rebuts, "I like ol' Joe. You'd wear anythin' you could find to if you's playin' football up there in all that snow. Poor feller's legs were cold!" he snapped in defence.

Frowning at his cousin and changing the subject, "What about our garden?" Johnny inquires, "Been down to check on it lately?"

"Oh yea!" Shannon answers with wide eyes, "It's doin' good!"

"OK, then. I'm about done here for today." Johnny, a spitting match for his father with his blue eyes and blond hair, exclaims with satisfaction.

"Wanna go huntin' tonight?" Shannon draws, "Now'd be a fine time with ol' Denny's truck outta commission."

Looking at his cousin as though he'd lost what little bit of sense he had to begin with, "Are you kiddin'?" Johnny protests, "That big bastard will probably be waitin' for us underneath some tree with a rifle. He's mighty pissed off at us right now."

Disappointed, Shannon whines, "Well... lemme know if you change ya mind."

Backing away from the motorcycle stand, John says in a slightly agitated tone, "Right now we gotta get to the feed store 'for I'm late for work." Lowering the tailgate for Skeeter to jump in the back of the old truck, Johnny then crawls up on the 5 gallon bucket. Shannon slides in the driver's seat, grumbling as he fires up the vehicle, "Sure could use our big timber back."

Snapping his head in Shannon's direction and shooting him a foul look, "You just achin' fer trouble ain't ya? You want the damn thing back? You go right on over and fetch it yourself." With a vigorous shake of his head, "I fer one don't wanna get my ass shot off!!!"

Sipping an old fashioned Coke float to wash down all that greasy beef, Porter turns to his partner asking, "Soooo.. Did that sheriff know anything that'll help us?"

"No!" the reporter gruffly answers. "At least he said he didn't. But something tells me he knows more than he's letting on." Recalling the conversation, she continues, "The way he looked at me... as if he was having a hard time holding something back he'd like to say. And that big game warden, it looked like he too was trying to avoid the conversation."

Raring back slightly and mocking, "That sheriff gave me the old, 'Honey.. I've heard those ol' rumours ever since I moved here', but he acted awful vague on most of my questions... as if he were doing his best to hide something. This all just seems a bit fishy to me."

Hearing enough, "That's what public officials do..." Porter informs, "they lie!" Standing from his stool to leave, "I've got to buy new batteries for my camera. The ones I bought from the office are stone cold dead so let's find a place that sells them and you can ask around there."

Lips slightly open and grinding a couple of teeth in frustration, sheriff Shift sits with Denny in his patrol car as they watch the cafe door open. The reporter and her assistant exit and head for their car.

"Lil missy there worries the shit outta me askin' 'bout all that." the sheriff says with heavy words, "Seems like every few years somebody comes nosin' 'round here lookin' for answers to questions I'd rather never mention again."

Nodding in agreement, Denny adds, "Now we know why ol' Cliff lit a shuck outta there like he did."

"Mmmm hmmm." Shift moans painfully, "Not good……."

Hearing a distinct rumble coming fast in their direction, Denny clenches his jaws tight, like a junkyard dog clutching onto a prize bone. A sound he's all too familiar with, it's the roar of the hemi engine in the Cochran boy's loud ass pickup truck. The same truck he was out chasing that caused so much trouble for him in the wee hours of the morning. "There them little bastards go!" the big man booms! Turning in time to see them race by in the other direction, glaring at his friend with a sour expression, the game warden blasts, "You know that goddamn truck won't pass inspection! Why do you let them assholes drive it around?"

"Cause if I diddn' let em drive it," Shift replies smugly, "they'd just get pissed off and tear up somethin' to spite me." Looking over at Denny with a bit of a smirk, "They ain't done nothin' all that bad, 'cept bruise your ego a little and fuck up the front end'a your truck." then changing his tone to a bit more scolding one, "but if I recall… it was you…ran over atop a that railroad post… not them." Denny begins to snort out a revolt but the sheriff halts him with an authoritative finger, "You ever heard'a the time those boys got into their grandpa's demolition equipment and made a homemade hand grenade?" Intrigued, Denny recants his rage and cracks a slight grin while shaking his head to the negative. "Sawed a Fram fuel filter in half," Shift recalls, "packed it with blastin' powder, screws and lock washers, then duct taped it back together with a fuse stickin' out."

Denny's grin is more relaxed as he anticipates the story and listens "Poor Shannon Ray musta missed whatever he was a throwin' the thing at. It bounced and rolled inta their grandpa's chicken coop. Well, thinkin' it was somethin' ta eat, all them chickens come runnin' toward it. 'Bout that time the son of a bitch blew up, shreddin' them chickens, blowin' chicken chum and feathers all over everywhere. Looked like a scene from a Hanna-Barbera cartoon. What chickens it diddn' kill, it maimed the rest. None of them chickens never did lay no more eggs after that."

Laughing to the point he can barely breathe, Denny's expression says it all. "Yep.." Shift continues, "their grandpa beat their ass, then worked em hard all summer ta pay for them chickens."

Obviously ready to comment, Denny spits, "And they diddn' learn nothin' from it neither!"

"Yes they did!" the sheriff calmly corrects, "They learned not ta get caught. Now, you really want me to piss them boys off by takin' their truck away from em?"

Denny thinks about that and after a few moments changes the subject back to the crisis at hand. "You know, regardin' our present predicament, rumour has it they took pictures back in the day before they buried him."

"Pictures...??" Shift repeats in awe. "Never heard that one before...

...well thank the gods nobody's ever seen em."

Drawing by Keith "Turtle" Cantoro, Monee, IL.

******

Chapter 13

Tintype

1897

Located north of Fort Worth between Rhome and Greasy Bend, the town of Aurora sat with a whopping total population of 372 people. It had its own furniture store, shoemaker shop, apothecary and blacksmith, but was too small for its own telegraph office. It did on the other hand have its own signal transmitter and receiver, setup in a back room of one of the two dry goods stores. Henry Daniel was the only man in town who could read the clicks and clacks of the instrument and he could do it well. With wide set violet eyes tilted between arched brows, a straight assertive nose, slightly cleft chin and a mouth a touch too wide, his features communicated a slight vulnerability as well as intelligence. If he was at his workstation, messages could come and go with ease, but if he was gone home for the day, good luck trying to get him back away from that wife of his.

Fortunately old Henry was just coming into work as Sheriff Otto brusquely dictated a message to the Texas Ranger station over in Fort Worth. In an attempt to explain the situation of the crash, its victim and the water problem, the telegrapher hunched over his clacking Morse code instrument and entered the sequence of taps. If the Rangers decided the event worthy of their attention, they would ride over and he'd show them the remains of the craft and the blown out tower. If not, he reckoned he would just have to make it on his own.

As for the pilot, he was gonna put him in the ground before nightfall. No matter what. Several had noticed a foul stench coming from his tiny cadaver. Not like the smell of a dead person, but more along the lines of a rancid fish and he'd been dead less than a day. No way Otto was going let him ripen overnight.

Moving at a brisk pace to return to the telegraph desk and see if there had been a reply from Fort Worth, heading inside the store and toward the back of the shop, Otto could hear excited words coming from Henry's little workstation. He knew that voice, S.E. Hayden, that over excited journalist feller who worked part time for the newspaper over in Dallas.

"No Dammit, I said *NOT* an inhabitant of this world! Can't you hear me?" Hayden was yelling at old Henry like he'd done stole one of his cows.

Quickening his step to see what the ruckus was about. "What's the trouble back here?" Otto asked sharply on his arrival.

"Sheriff!" cried the telegrapher, "Hayden's been here damn near an hour demandin' fer'me ta signal his news story! I got other things ta do!"

"Sheriff!" Hayden interrupted, "This is an important moment! A day not to be forgot around these parts! Now you tell this old fool to…"

"I've no intention of tellin' Mr. Daniel anythin'!" Otto scolded.

"Oh come on sheriff!" the reporter spat.

"Nothin' doin'! You may get paid for your ink slingin' over in the big city but the rest of us don't hafta put up with you bein' so damned ornery cause a it! Now you give ol' Henry here time to do what he needs and maybe, just maybe, if you can control your temper... he'll click out your report. You should'a…"

Otto continued, but Hayden had heard enough and stormed past him toward the front of the store uttering a variety of insults and heading for the boardwalk.

Hayden was so fired up over the incredible early morning happenings that he'd completely lost his head. One of Aurora's biggest cotton buyers, he didn't normally behave like that but in his excitement to get news of the event to his superiors he'd overstepped himself.

Laying a hand on the signal operator's shoulder, "Henry, our mamas never told us they'd be days like this." then with a heavy sigh, "Tryin' times for us all. Don't take it personal. He's doin' his job like we're tryin' ta do ours and he diddn' mean ta be a horse's ass." Henry nodded.

"Now," the sheriff continued, "have you heard back from the rangers?"

Nodding once more, Daniels confirmed, "Said ta tell ya they'd be here tomorrow sometime." Otto patted the telegrapher again, gave him a nod of thanks and headed for the street.

Emerging onto the boardwalk, the sheriff glanced up to see the sun more than halfway past its zenith and a crowd of people gathered across the street in front of his office. Growling under his breath, the last thing he wanted today was to see more excitement in his town. There'd already been more drama today since the great fire and now folks was pouring into town by the wagon load to get a look at the dead airship being. "What'n blazes is this?" he shouted while approaching the group, all but pushing his way through the crowd of onlookers. There he was, the poor deceased alien in his pitch covered coffin, now wearing a badly worn gambler's hat. A truly pitiful sight, he'd been hauled outside and propped up in the daylight. Put on display up along the boardwalk for all to see, exposure to the suns rays only hastened his decomposition.

"Documentin' the event, sheriff," prompted a man standing behind an immense camera with the dark cloth over his head, "...come over and get in!"

"Well I be damned!" Otto protested, "Ain't none'a y'all got nothin' better to do? It appears to me, he needs buryin' lot more'n he needs a tintype!"

Surprisingly enough it had been Doc Sam's idea. So many folks had barged into his office begging to see the creature that he decided to solve the problem. For the sake of history, his nephew owned a fancy new Kodak and had been wanting to use it for some occasion other than weddings, funerals, family reunions or outlaw groups seeking portraits.

Wandering into town for a visit and hearing the news, his nephew had hurried back home, loaded the picture machine, a 4×5 inch Model C Kodak daylight. Gathering it and three 4×5 inch exposure holders with various other equipment and a tripod to mount it all on, he'd wasted no time in loading said equipment on his buckboard. Lashing it securely, he headed back to town. Setting up the apparatus off the boardwalk for the unprecedented occasion, he got behind the covered viewfinder to adjust the focus just as Otto came into his frame. "It's for the periodical." responded the cameraman with an edge of determination. "And it's not a tintype. It's a daguerreotype."

"Wretched scandal sheet! I don't give a damn what your depiction plates called!" Otto scolded, "Taint right!" looking at the dead creature in the box, "and for Christ's sake, who put the bloody hat on em?"

"I did sheriff…" came a voice from the crowd. After stitching up Miss Wilkinson's foot and getting rid of S.E. Hayden, Doc Sam had sent word to everybody who'd first ran to the crash to meet here and have their portrait taken with the little traveler who dropped out of the sky and met his unfortunate demise in their fair town. Now dressed in his Sunday best, he was escorting Jenni herself toward the scene. Stopping back by the hotel, Jenni had washed up a bit and then changed into her best little dusty rose traveling outfit with matching hat.

"Well... it don't seem fittin'... that's all!" the sheriff grumbled over his concerns with the tattered topper, "He ain't from around here! Probably ain't never even seen a hat... much less put one on!" Frowning with distaste at the entire affair. "See you got your six dollar suit on, aye doc?" ribbed the exhausted lawman to the sight of the town physician locked arms with the town whore strolling along side by side to have their beauty struck, "Gettin' a mite tight ain't it?"

"Alright sheriff... calm down, you win." Sam replied to the badgering as he moved toward the coffin. Giving in to Otto's displeasure and removing the hat from the cadaver. "Happy now?" he asked mockingly. Otto said nothing.

"Can I sit down?" asked Jenni.

"No!" the photographer barked from behind the dark cloth.

"But my foot hurts!" she countered.

"Iffin you want in the shot you gotta stand!"

"Hey!" snapped the cameraman when a Mexican drifter wandered into the frame and stopped, "No chilli-pickers, darkies, or redskins in the portrait!"

"Mercy sakes, I coulda' told ya that." spat Mona with a laugh at the very notion and who'd just walked up, returning from Sven's farm to crowded streets and talk of a tintype. Fanning herself beside the coffin as the Mexican gave her a look and continued on; she had also changed into her finest outfit and was excited to have her portrait make, with or without the dead critter from outer space. "Can't we get on with this?" she protested while wrinkling her nose at the foul odor emanating from the creature, "The devil smells to high heaven."

"That little feller can't help it." remarked her roommate, "There's times you don't smell much like no flower garden neither." then with a frown to the man taking too much time behind the Kodak, "and yes, can we please get on with this? I'm gettin' a sunburn!"

Ignoring the comment from her roommate, "First time ever got myself a tintype." Mona said more or less to herself because no one else in attendance would have cared. "Next I'll be goin' ta church on Sunday."

Ruffling her hair Jenni ribbed, "Look who's talkin'." while several others looked on dryly with no response.

Putting on a hoity toity attitude, Mona began "I'm not the one…"

Only to be cut off by the widow Herzkee, walking onto the scene with a freshly baked cake for the festivities, "Should we?" she prompted.

"Cake!" clapped Jenni "I vote yes!"

"I vote yes." said the Doc. He loved cake.

Vonetta McGee, strolling to the event after spotting her two friends, spoke up, "What we votin' for?"

"Cake!" explained the widow.

"A definite yes!" answered Vonetta, "I'll help serve."

"This ain't no party!" Sheriff Otto grumbled, "Can't we get on with this?"

"Hey that's not for …" Mr. Kodak snapped, when Vern drug the step stool away from his side.

"Well I diddn' mean fer ya ta get put out none. Whatta ya spect me ta do," the drunk cried, "I'm plum tuckered out"

"Go ahead'n sit on it." was Otto's suggestion.

"The cake?" Vonetta cried, "Don't you dare!"

"God help me." muttered Vern, sinking fast.

"Least the rain held off." someone cracked.

"Jesus... will y'all shut up?" there again grumbled the man behind the Kodak, "You's all look like you're headin' to a funeral"

"We are dammit," cried Otto, "Now take the cussed picture!"

Rarely ever was there occasion for a portrait. Women wore their best clothes and the men stood erect holding their weapons, while the tiny figure in the coffin was silent.

1897 Aurora Texas Body Unknown

Just as the photographer loaded and exposed his third and last plate. The gathering was interrupted by a spectacle that would go down in history as one of the most bizarre sights ever beheld in the American West. It looked like a scene right out of *Gulliver's Travels*. The remains of the crumpled alien ship, a stellar means of transportation from another world capable of flying some millions of miles through space, being dragged by a horse drawn wagon down the street with the deputy and the cowboy out in front.

A once magnificent galactic vessel capable of skipping across the solar system now reduced to a dead heap of twisted metal and torn fragments. Slightly closer to the spacecraft and on each side of the wagon, two mules, each led by one of Sven's boys, tethered and pulling slowly in unison. All straining and tugging while Sven sat atop the wagon making sure everything went according to his plan.

Quickly sizing up the situation at the windmill site, Sven envisioned the people of Troy dragging the giant wooden horse through its streets. Using every rope he could get his hands on, they expertly webbed the crumpled vessel into a net. Running leads to tie into the web, 10 minutes later two flop eared mules and two horses were hitched to the wagon and they all began to grunt and tug for all their worth as a pair of fiendish looking turkey vultures sat on bare tree limbs looking on.

Once they'd dug out some of the mud and gotten the downed machine out of the hole created beneath the soggy remains of the tower, the group manoeuvred the craft to lie on its smooth belly. Surprisingly light for its size, the ropes strained but held as the hull slid along the flat landscape. Dragging the silver spaceship down the hill and through the main street, the parade through Aurora was a once in a lifetime sight and everyone gathered along the street seemed to know it.

News had traveled fast and spectators from all of Wise County had converged on Aurora. A volatile mix of loafers loafing and gawkers gawking, crowded the street. Horses tethered to flatbed wagons and along fences shimmied nervously as the hulking dead machine moved by.

Sven tipped his hat with a slight grin to the sheriff as the parade passed by. Their small town had seen some strange times, Otto thought, but group portraits with an alien traveler and this curious sight struggling and grappling through the dusty street took the cake.

After all this, Aurora, Texas would never be the same.

******

Chapter 14

Delicious

1997

Dominated by banks, pawn shops and lending services for folks with bad credit, by 1997 Aurora, Texas bore no resemblance to its former self of the 1890s. Located in an abandoned filling station for several decades, the Wise County Sheriff's headquarters consisted of two tiny offices and one overcrowded room where the police band radio equipment was situated.

The dispatcher, who also served double duty as file clerk and receptionist for incoming traffic, was someone who certainly had their hands full. Forced to entertain every kook and crazy who ran inside, there was a steady stream of trivial complaints such as, "Maylon just crashed into my new truck" or "Larry done runoff with my youngest daughter." Also responsible for taking fire calls, the building was 30 by 40 feet long and the fire department was a poker table set up in the station's wash bay where they kept the city's aging fire truck.

If ever there was a scene that rivalled anything presented on a vintage episode of the *Keystone Kops*, Aurora's fire department was sure to please. Anything that caught fire usually wound up an inferno by the time the volunteer department rallied and eventually made its way to the scene. When that bright red phone began to ring inside the office, it was the damnedest thing you ever did see. Straight out of *It's a Mad Mad Mad Mad World*, volunteers raced to the firehouse, coming down the street on the wrong side, screeching into the parking lot on two wheels, jumping curbs and running over the sidewalk. Sometimes even crashing into one another or the department flag pole. All in a desperate attempt to be the first to arrive and get behind the wheel of the fire truck, they slipped and slid to a stop wherever they landed. Several times they had to repair the building from pickups crashing into its side.

The local feed and seed store is one of the busiest places in town. Supplying a whopping 35-40 customers per day, they sell everything from lumber, stored in a great tall building a hundred feet from the main entrance, to building materials, farming supplies and of course animal feed by the sack full. Most anything the good townspeople may need on a daily basis.

Taking a part time job there back in the fall to give the appearance that at least one of the cousins had a legitimate job; Johnny feared it may look a tad suspicious if they both did whatever they liked without any source of real income to fund their exploits. Dropped off by Shannon, Johnny gets directly to work inside until noticing an unfamiliar vehicle pulling into the parking lot.

Not your average farm truck with bent fenders and multicolored doors, this slick black Olds was an eye catcher, not to mention the adorable young lady in the passenger seat. Letting out a low uncontrollable whistle from his side of the store window, he watches as our pretty correspondent steps out and approached the building.

Observing a pair of town's finest roosting in the shade on the dead dick bench, Bonnie makes an introduction as Porter goes inside, "Afternoon gents…" standing over the elderly gentleman a mere three feet away, "I'm

Bonnie Reynolds from the *Gainesville Daily Register*. I'm trying to do a follow-up story on a hundred year old article about a craft that crashed into the local water reserve." Bowing slightly to flash a bit of cleavage and a bright smile, she asks, "Either of you handsome fellas ever heard of it?"

"I heard of it?" they both say at about the same time.

Her interest instantly piqued and now feeling a touch more confident, "Okay then…" she chirps amusingly as if talking to a pair of children, "tell me what you know."

"Ain't too much ta tell darlin'…" the one on the right says, then stops to spit a stream of tobacco juice on the ground beside him. Gathering his thoughts for a moment, "Story goes there's this little short feller whacked it in a silver looking bowl. Got caught'n a windstorm and blowed the top outta the old water tank." Taking another spit and catching another breath, "Said he died… like this town 'bout died when the depression hit. Everthin' from back in them days is gone now. No more'n a couple die hard farmers and ranchers stayed durin' them tough times." then after pausing momentarily to draw another breath, "Pretty much sugar, if you diddn' have a way ta feed your family… you left."

Absorbing the old man's account, Bonnie asks, "So…. are there any of those 'die hard' relatives still living around here?"

"Oh, Yeah!" the old codger nods, "There's the Cochrans, Stuarts, the Chotes, the Shifts…"

"Shift?" the reporter quickly interrupts. "You don't mean the sheriff?"

"Yeaaah." the old man drawled with a puzzled look, "Know 'em do ya?" She knew him alright, knew that he'd lied to her face earlier in the morning. Saying that he had moved here from somewhere else and acting all stupid to her questions. Biting her lip with anger but trying desperately not to show it, "I met him this morning along with the game warden." she answers calmly.

"Denny?" cracks the old man, "Hee hee, everybody seems ta like ol' Denny. His folks was 'round here back in them days."

All of a sudden she was thankful that Porter had grabbed the wrong batteries. This old man was providing a wealth of information. Watching and listening from inside, Johnny becomes enthralled in the exchange going on between the two. So was someone else.

Unperceived, the shifty sales clerk behind the feed store counter minding the cash drawer is taking in every word said… with very different intentions.

Removing a dirty ball cap embossed with an out of business oil company logo and wiping the sweat from his head with the long sleeve of his shirt, the elderly chap who's been so talkative yodel, "Ya know… ol' Vickers was goin' 'round tellin' folks one time that his daddy done stole a piece'a it the day it went down when he was a youngin."

Eyes big as saucers after hearing the mention of his grandpa Vickers name, somewhere in the back of his mind Johnny recalls hearing something spoken by relatives to that effect so long ago he'd plum forgot about it… until now.

Holding his silence for as long as possible, the second codger on the bench outside the store now perks up and has his say, "You can't believe that bullshit! Everybody 'round here knows ol' Vickers is a liar! He made up that story like everythin' else comes outta his mouth!"

Johnny's face turns three shades of red hearing his grandfather spoken of in such a manner. He didn't like that old coot worth a damn to begin with but in an effort to hear more about the situation, he holds his temper and continues to listen.

Greatly interested in this titbit of information, "Who's 'old Vickers?'" Bonnie asks.

Still chatty, the first codger who'd been such a help explains, "That's Johnny Dale's grandpa…" after a quick wipe with his shirt sleeve to remove the dribble from his chin, "see young John's daddy went ta school with Denny. They was best friends. Then when John's daddy was killed in the service, he went to live with his grandpa Vickers."

Still somewhat confused but struggling to see the greater picture, Miss Reynolds asks, "So… where can I find this Johnny Dale?"

"Ohhhh…" cried the oldster, "That's the boy works here! He's inside right now!" Johnny almost falls to his knees.

Sliding the gas powered hedge trimmer, rakes and gas can forward in the bed of the city owned maintenance truck, Clarence loads several sacks of fertilizer purchased on its rotating municipal account. All the while paying attention to the exchange of conversation between the young lady and the old men, the groundskeeper listened carefully to the history lesson knowing that his uncle would also be interested. Closing the tailgate, he leaves as Bonnie thanks the old man for his help and heads for the door of the store.

Removing her sunglasses as she enters the dimly lit building, her breath catches at the sight of the young man before her. What was that she thought. You never act like this when you see a guy. Suck it up girl! "Johnny Dale, I presume?" she flairs spotting her prey who has a deer in the headlights expression. Studying him like a hungry wolf studies a flop eared jackrabbit; he looked simply delicious in his worn boots and cut off flannel shirt.

Don't you dare flinch and reveal what you're thinking she told herself strutting in front of the boy, this time she decided her approach would be much different. "Hello charming." she reaches and flips his shoulder length hair back with a look of arousal, "Gramps outside forgot to mention how cute you were."

His eyes glued on her, at first she seemed to have had a quizzical look. He'd never seen this girl before but felt drawn to her like a magnet. Not since his days with Reagan had he felt these types of feelings and it scared the living hell out of him. He'd vowed to never let such emotions ever control him again. "I…I don't know nothin' 'bout none'a that."

"Ahhhhhh…" she pouts with puckered lips. "Is that all you think I want?" Slowly moving forward, she now backs him into a corner.

"I reckon so." he rasps, sounding almost like a grunt. Stopping so close she can feel the heat of his presence and smell of his scent, her senses reeled. Damn, she wasn't prepared for this.

Reaching up, she takes hold of the top button of his plaid shirt and pulls his face slowly down to hers. "Well, that's what you get for thinking." she softly whispers, kissing him gently on the lips. His mere touch sent frizzles soaring through her. She wanted to shake her head to clear these illicit thoughts but couldn't dare let him see the vulnerability.

Stuttering a bit, "I… st-still don't know nothin'" he groans.

"Nothing?" she coaxes, bowing her head slightly with a whimsical look that lets him know she doesn't believe him for a second.

Wanting to speak his peace he snaps, "I know my grandpa ain't no liar!"

Reaching without hesitation for the top button once more and pulling him close, before releasing him and strolling casually out of the store, she rests her cheek beside his and whispers, "Then help me prove it…"

******

Chapter 15

Darkness

1897

Descended from a group of Swedish immigrants that settled in the West during the 1850s, 57 year old Sven Johansson was a deeply spiritual man. Tall and lanky, standing a shade over 6 feet without his boots, he had heavily shaded eyebrows and a thick thatch of unruly salt and pepper hair under a tattered wide-brim floppy hat which shaded his clear blue eyes.

An avid Bible reader, Sven recalled its stories of *"celestial gods who descended to earth in their brightly colored flying ships"* so having one of his boys take the wagon reins, he took a moment to detour from the parade and get a closer look at this feller who'd supposedly fell from the heavens. Didn't look nothing at all like no God he'd ever read about, not that he'd ever actually seen one in person. Baffled by the looks of the pilot in shiny cloths propped up in the small cedar coffin, this creature didn't fit the any of the stereotype profiles he'd read about in the testaments. God and his followers were believed to resemble Herculean figures capable of hurling thunderbolts and able to control the seas. Greatly confused by the small penguin like figure with reptilian skin and the eyes of a monstrous insect, all he could conclude of the pilot who'd gotten himself killed in the crash was that he must have been a servant of the gods who had escaped in one of their vessels. A minion from heaven.

With the collective efforts of Sven, his boys, his mules, Harland, Frenchie and their horses, they'd drug the crumpled craft through the streets of town and to the livery stable with still over an hour of daylight remaining.

On the opposite side of town from where the crash had happened, in the world of livery stables throughout the Lone Star State, many are well kept, others decent, some downright disgusting. Few who may have traveled across the plains of Texas and happen to stay overnight in Aurora had ever seen one as well kept as wicked Wanda's.

Wearily munching hay in their stables, several horses stomped disapprovingly at the sight of the twisted metal beast entering their space as the craft came to rest inside the huge barn. Snorting nervously, they bared their teeth and shook their head from side to side; forming an unruly background chorus as if to shout, "Don't bring that damn thing in here!" In unison with the animals, a ragged voice came from behind the tuckered out deputy, "OH NO! You's ain't bringin' that damn thang in here!"

Wanda Crabtree was the owner of the Livery Stables. Folks who didn't know her were shocked to find that some crazy fool had ever got naked and laid down to father anything with her, ugly as she was. Built like a man, a rough looking man at best, this cuss of a woman had jowls that sagged about as bad as her chest and her eyes bulged worse than a toad's.

She could put some pretty decent grub on the table but even so that didn't make up for that twisted face she barked from. Dressed in men's work duds and constantly gnawing a thin cigarillo, she packed not one but double shooting iron from both hips. Smith & Wesson .44 Russians. Not someone to mess with.

What inevitably made her so damned ornery was puttin' up with them two boys of hers. At 8 years old they were both wide open playing cowboys and Indians. Course half-breed was always stuck playing the redskin. Banging away at one another with old rusty cap and ball Colts and sneaking away to the swimming hole, they'd tease the other, "That water's gonna feel mighty good!"

Now in their late teens and into all manners of devilment, their weakness was girls. Horney jackpots they was. Went through them like oats in the horse bend. Their ma had caught them in the top of the haymow, rolling in the hay with half of the young fillies in town. Sometimes two at a time. Warning there'd be the devil to pay if one of them girls turned up bloated because of them, Wanda would whip 'em best she could, which was pretty bad tough as old Wanda was, but they'd just go right back and do it again the next day like she'd never said a word. No matter how much of a stink she made, Wanda couldn' keep the females away. They were always hanging out at her stables and none of them girls had no horse of their own.

The boys tended to dress like dandies. Jake, known collectively throughout town as "half-breed" had a fancy buckskin coat with gold fringe. Tyler wore bright silky vests with a red kerchief at his throat. Both boys' daddies were dandies too.

Half-breeds daddy was an Indian that the boy had never met and never would. Tyler's daddy stayed with Wanda for a couple years but during the time drunk himself to death. Told everybody it was because Wanda was so rough on him, "*wretched cuss of a woman with a foul mouth and an iron fist.*" he'd say.

Carefully trying not to rile her now, "Sheriff says it stays till he decides different." Frenchie replied of the twisted spaceship now resting in her barn.

"Takes up too much room!" she screeched while shaking her head from side to side, "and it's a scarin' my horses!"

"And... he wants a cover throwed over it." the deputy added waiting for a violent reply.

"Cover?" Wanda snapped, "Well fuck me sideways!" she dismissed in disbelief, "Ain't like the dratted thangs gonna get up'n run-off!"

"Wanda…" the deputy began to plead.

"Don't Wanda me! Whatta I look like?" she interrupted, knowing only too well what she looked like, "and who's gonna pay fer it to stay?"

Frenchie didn't have a precise answer for that one. Moving his lips from side to side and kicking the dirt with his boot, "Town I reckon?" he stammered.

"Town already owes me six dollars!" the stable owner dismissed with a violent shake, "Has fer over two months now!"

"Dammit!" Frenchie started, "I'm just tellin' ya what…."

"I need these stalls for horses belongin' to payin' customers!"

"Looks ta me like you ain't got no payin' customers…" Frenchie calmly countered looking around the barn, "Ever' horse I see in here belongs ta you Wanda."

Just as the old gal balled up her fists and started to spit something foul mouthed back, the deputy held up his hands and continued, "Now look, you ain't gotta rub it down nor feed it, so let it sit here a day or so!" Wearing down, the ornery livery lady pursed her lips into a snarl but stayed quiet. "Don't fret, next time sheriff fines somebody that's got money I'm sure he'll make it a tad steeper and send it over."

"If he fines em!" she spat, "Cause he usually don't!"

"Wanda!" the deputy twitched with burning irritation.

"Alright!" she spat begrudgingly, "Two days … then it's gotta go!"

"Much obliged." Smiling thinly as he touched two fingers to the brim of his hat, he didn't mean it, not to this nightmare of a woman.

Staring at the craft and rocking with steaming frustration on the heels of her boots, "This is bull shit!" she barked belligerently while looking at the twisted wreckage.

"Awwww now… quit your bellyachin'." he reassured, "You'll get paid."

"You'll get paid!" she mocked with a now haggard tone demanding to know, "Where's Otto at anyways?"

"Out the cemetery…" the deputy sighed, worn out from the beratement and nodding toward the remains of the craft, "Buryin' the feller come outta that."

Warm shadows lengthened as the Texas sun made its descent. A chill creeping into the air became evident as the last rays of the day's natural light began to vanish in the west. Following the spectacles on the boardwalk and in the street, the lid had been nailed in place on the small coffin belonging to the strange feller who had so disrupted the small town on April, 17th.

A small procession including both girls who'd been first on the scene, Vern, Sam and a few onlookers made its way to the cemetery behind a buckboard guided by Roberto, Otto and none other than the drifter who'd witnessed the crash.

Appropriately enough it was the cowboy who dumped the first shovel full of earth atop the grave and Otto who spoke a few kind words on the small gray skinned traveler's behalf. "Lord..." he began with his hat in his hand, "We know we're not your best'a servants, but we do try and we do the best we can. None of us don't rightly know just what this little feller is or where he's from, but do know is he met his unfortunate end here in our town, so we did the best for him we could. Now we'd appreciate if you could see to give him a break and do your best for him…whoever he may be. Amen."

By the time darkness fell that evening, on a small knoll far in the eastern corner of the graveyard, a freshly covered mound of earth was topped with a specially scribed wooden cross. The tiny alien would remain in this hastily dug grave of consecrated ground, trapped light years from his home in a place he had never known. Shoved into the ground at the head of the plot, deeply etched into the marker atop his final resting place was a single word. Different from any others in the yard, it read,

TRAVELER.

******

Chapter 16

UFO

1997

Slipping back to the store office, following the exchange between the young reporter and the young employee, 39 year old sales clerk Ralph Embrey punches numbers into a phone. Ringing up Porter's batteries, chips, candy and latest edition *X-Men* comic book he'd paid particular attention to the man's press credentials, as well as the conversation playing out in the corner. "Houston, we have a problem." he quips into the receiver.

"Very funny." an un-amused voice on the other end growls, "What the fuck do you want?"

"Well now… always a pleasure to hear from you too there ace." Ralph taunts his superior. "There's this young reporter snooping around over here asking lots of questions about that little incident that cost you your job."

"Yea, so?" the voice grumbles. Interested, but hesitant to become too interested, "What do you want from me?"

"Soooo… *she* looks a whole lot better that you ever thought about and folks are talking..." he injects with a certain ring in his tone that makes the agent sit up a little straighter in his chair. During the exchange, Ralph peeps out of the cluttered office window at Porter and Bonnie as they get into the Oldsmobile to leave. Continuing with the agent in a whiny voice, "I got one of them not so fresh feelings about this."

"I know about your not so fresh feelings." FBI agent Mike Travers replies condescendingly. Rising from his office chair, he walks across the room to one of three filing cabinets. "You remember what happened last time," he says while retrieving a file from the center one and returning to his desk. "I'm not coming over there again to get my chain yanked by those jokers." Back in his chair he opens a heavily marked on file titled, *Aurora*. A file he wishes he could simply forget.

"Okay... okay... don't do nothing." the informant dismisses, "Tell you what... just forget I called."

"You know those hick bastards are the reason I'm behind this desk." Travers reminds his informant while flipping through the file.

"I'm following orders," the snitch says in defence, "and my orders are to report any developments concerning the... mystery. Just thought I'd let you know before filling out a report." he continues in a tempting tone, "Never know, something may just come out to help get your position back?"

Thinking that last statement over for a moment, Travers grumbles once more, "Alright you dirty bastard, you had better be right... I'll be on my way within the hour. Now keep this quiet! Oh... and this reporter, which paper did you say she worked for?"

At the *Gainesville Daily Register,* the relationship between Bonnie and her editor has always been cordial and professional. For a boss who some regarded as a tyrant, he believed the ambitious journalist had the makings of a fine reporter. One who might even someday move up to TV news. The only way to fly.

City editor by profession, bilious grouch by disposition, Rodney Grail was tough and expected the best from his staff. They are after all the heart of his newspaper, if he couldn't keep the bloodline pumping to his extremities in order to keep them motivated, what good were they? Firing nearly as many as he'd hired, one had quit in a rage throwing a snow globe taken from the editor's desk, a souvenir from the National UFO Museum in Roswell, New Mexico, through a frosted office window before storming out of the building. But Grail was a fair man; he gave as good as he got in return.

Millie in accounting had worked for him for over 6 years, never once complaining about him as a boss. Sure he was a bit gruff but never acted nasty to her. The reason was simple; she did her job without having to be watched over. For someone strapped with such a stressful managerial position, he could have been far worse. In her eyes his snapping and barking was as harmless as an old hound who knew no other way to communicate.

Standing beside one of his employees seated at their desk, looking over their work and scolding them about the importance of credibility in a newsman, Grail was alerted by his secretary of a call waiting on line 4.

"Mr. Grail," an arrogant voice begins, "This is FBI agent Mike Travers of the Fort Worth bureau, I understand you have a young lady over in Aurora making inquiries on a matter which is still part of an ongoing investigation with our department."

"What's it to you?" the editor thunders to the pompous ass, "Until this morning I'd never heard anything about it?"

"I want to inform you sir," Travers continues unaffected, "that anything she may uncover concerning the incident is subject to my discretion and you are hereby ordered to inform me before printing or releasing any information on the matter. Is that clear?'"

With his free arm folded across his chest and clutching his other arm to have something to cling to, Grail stares forward with a small smile of resistance, "Hereby ordered?" he injects with almost a laugh. Knowing that he is obligated for nothing.

"That is correct sir," the agent retorts, "I advise your best course of action would be to recall her at once. But if you chose otherwise, I insist you take my number and report to me immediately with any information she may uncover."

"Well I appreciate your advisement sir," the editor lies with a sinister expression, "I'll be delighted to contact you with any updates agent… Travers." Writing the name on a scrap sheet of paper, he's not going to report a damn thing to this creep regardless of his position but plays along for good measure. Following a moment of scribbling, he slams down the phone and picks up the paper. It read: *Agent Travers, 863-ASS-HOLE!*

In the Old West the only dire necessity second to a man's horse was his gun. In its time, the 1873 Winchester was referred to as "the gun that won the west." Equally popular was Samuel Colt's Peacemaker, an early cartridge load revolver which allowed six shots to be fired from a single cylinder. Quickly reloadable and ready to fire again, it thus revolutionized the firearms industry.

Hand drawn wanted posters (dodgers as commonly referred to in the past) had long been replaced with machine printouts of "*Wanted for the arrest and conviction of*" rather than the previous and more explicit "*WANTED: DEAD OR ALIVE*". Sheriff Shift brushed by several of these new style posters on the way to his desk. A traditionalist who has the greatest respect for history, he wears on his side, not one of the modern 9mm semi-automatic cookie cutter pistols, but a tough and proven early 1900s Colt single action nickel plated .45.

The morning had proven to be more stressful than normal between Denny's misadventure and facing that feline reporter. For the first time today he manages to ease into the chair at his desk, check his mail and return a few phone calls. Just as he opens and begins to read an expected letter, the door of his office bursts open.

"You lied to me!" Miss Reynolds screeches like a pissed off exotic bird.

"I told her you were busy sir!" his secretary injects from behind the reporter.

"It's alright Sheila." Shift concedes from his desk and knowing he's in for a fight.

"I'm sorry but she…" the secretary persists.

"It's alright Sheila!" he insists once more as the reporter stands silent but fuming. Upon the office assistants retreat, Bonnie slams the door with a scorned look and marches right over to the sheriff's desk. Uninhibited about speaking to this man in a way that most would think twice or even three times about, angry hands form fists which are firmly planted on her hips. Rising slowly from his chair, palms up in the please don't shoot me stance, he calmly counters, "Woo, woo, woo, wait a minute darlin'…"

Cutting him off quick, "Don't you darlin' me!" she snaps. "Would you like to explain why you felt it necessary to lie? To blatantly deceive me regarding your history in this town?"

Putting on his best fake grin in an effort to try and defuse the situation, he laughingly says "Well… I ain't lived here my *whole* life." focusing greatly on the word whole.

"Pfffft! Don't you give me that crap!" the reporter hisses, "You know precisely what I mean!" Failing her arms as the sheriff's grin falls away, "You know a lot more about this story than you're letting on and for whatever reason tried to brush me right to the side!"

Dancing around the subject with this spitfire is pointless. Shift lowers his head, shaking it from side to side and rubbing his throbbing temple with his fingers, "Miss Reynolds…" he begins, hardly knowing where to begin, "you're askin' questions 'bout somethin' like it or not, is better off not talked about around here."

"I knew it!" the reporter shrieks before taking a deep breath to continue, but the lawman silences her with an authoritative finger. His first real *don't mess with me woman* expression before going on.

"There's still a lotta hard feelin's after them government assholes came through here last time."

"What government assholes? What's that got to do with...?" Bonnie retorts, trailing off with a baffled look as the realization becomes apparent of what she's actually stumbled upon. "So, the story *is* true." she whispers mysteriously and feeling a touch week in the knees.

Thinking how to downplay the matter, Shift says rather sadly, "I'm sorry Miss Reynolds but this town don't need no more UFO stories."

"I didn't say UFO" Bonnie insists, crossing her arms. "You said UFO.!" then with a mock defence referring to the feds, adds "*THEY*… said UFO!"

Up to his eyeballs with the matter not to mention this vexing woman, the sheriff pleads, "We really shouldn' even be havin' this conversation."

"What-ever!" she dismisses with a laugh.

Realizing that he's already said far too much concerning the matter, "You best oughta let this one go and head on back to Gainesville."

With a retaliatory, you can't be serious laugh, "Ohhh, I'm going back all right!" she hisses, tugging the now worse for wear 1897 article from her bag. Shaking it with the stamina for confrontation she concludes, "Next week is the 100th anniversary of the story and I'm going to write my follow up with or without your help based on everything I've seen and heard here." emphasizing heavily, "You can be sure of that!"

Cutting her performance short, the sheriff injects, "Ma'am, you're not hearing me. Official Government Stance on this thing is that Nothin'... Ever... HAPPENED!" continuing harshly, "That it was all a hoax, made up back then ta try'n save a dyin' town! Now dammit all, that's what I hafta stick with!"

Holding out his hands now like a street beggar begging for loose change, "Take it or leave it, that's a direct order from Colonel Alexander over at Carswell Air Force Base."

Now in a silent standoff, the two strong willed patrons stand facing each other and glare. Who will win?

******

Chapter 17

Epidemic

1897

News spread throughout the day of the early morning incident in Aurora and the Texas Rangers were on their way to investigate. As twilight came, groups of folks from across the valley had been arriving in town all afternoon hoping to get a look at the small man from the heavens killed in the crash. They'd always considered God the only one that came from the heavens. The same God who everybody bowed their heads to and begged for help in times of need, only to be ignored. Now more than ever, they began to wonder.

The brightest full moon anyone could ever remember had just crept out from behind a bank of clouds in the crisp night air as flickers of lamp light threw long spooky shadows on store fronts and the street. Any poor soul throughout the region unfortunate enough to be stricken with lycanthropy would surely be turning now in the conundrum of its eerie rays.

The only sound in the cool night breeze was the chirping of locusts scraping their legs together. Every man, woman and beast was on edge. In the half-light made by the lamps within buildings and on the boardwalks, town's folk stood silently staring skyward. A carriage running late rolled to a stop in the dusty street as the driver craned his crooked neck upward, mimicking those around him. Out from the coach stepped Judge Proctor, pillar of the community and second in command. Oblivious to the strange happenings in town during his absence, he would soon learn what all the fuss was about and what had happened on his property and to his beloved flower garden while he'd been away on business.

Loafers on the porch in front of the dry goods store looked up appraisingly. Huddled outside in groups, fearing that they may now have more trouble than they could handle, an unsteady crowd was beginning to gather. They talked in hushed tones, some too drunk to see much of anything, trying to get a handle on what had happened in the early morning as they stared toward the night sky. Even the dogs were watching.

Lynn Davis, sweet as the pies she made, poured coffee from a battered pot which took permanent residence on the corner stove of the sheriff's office as the lawman's best hunting dog sniffed in her direction to be sure it wasn't a morsel intended for him. Sweet on the town's number one peace officer for quite some time, Otto didn't have to worry about a diet of leftover greasy beans and cold tortillas from across the street in the cantina. Like him, Lynn had lost her beloved during the spotted fever epidemic and for the past few years both widow and widower had been taking care of each other.

Filling two tin mugs with the steaming bitter brew, she was delighted to join him at his desk for a rather late supper. Following the exhausting events the day had delivered, she'd proudly prepared a fresh cauldron of chicken and dumplings for her man and bakes a crab apple cobbler for dessert. She even brought a small tin filled with cookies. Standing 5 foot 2 inches and about 4 years older than Otto, just as pretty as she was 20 years earlier, Lynn had medium length golden hair and the prettiest green eyes of any woman to ever come out of West Virginia.

Looking forward to a hot meal in the company of his number one lady, not to mention grinning for the first time since this crazy day had started,

"Lynn," he began kindly under the dim kerosene office lamp, "You'll never know how fine this suits me after the day I've had.""Now don't you fret over all this." resting her hand on his, her kind words provided some much needed reassurance. "Nothin' you nor anyone else could'a done that you didn't."

At 5 foot 9 inches without his boots on, Otto was a man who wore brightly colored shirts beneath several layers of black including a tailor made leather vest and black Stetson laden with silver conchos held in place by a thin leather band. Quite the muscular bulldog of a man even into his 50s, his dark hair and moustache were deeply blended with silver.

Opening his bottom desk drawer and retrieving a seldom used bottle of above average brandy, he added a dollop to not only his cup but hers as well with no protest from the lady who knew more sordid details concerning his past than anyone else in town. For this man had experienced far worse than anyone could imagine or begin to comprehend.

Visions were burned into his brain from the night Comanche savages attacked the campsite in which his family was a part of in the fall of 1851. Women screaming, children running for their lives, huts being ripped apart and set afire. Redskin murderers screaming war cries and death chants, slashing and hacking at the dying with crude axes. Slathered in warm blood, lapping it up with their tongues like thirst crazed beasts, they decapitated and scalped those who knelt for mercy.

With no provocation or warning, a small band of half-naked warriors wearing animal skins, yellowish brown face paint and scalps from recently slaughter victims had mounted themselves and suddenly descended on the small encampment sending unsuspecting waves of arrows and bullets from out of nowhere. By the time the men had readied themselves, fumbling in the dark and searching for their rifles, the siege had overwhelmed them with the element of surprise. Shot down one by one with plundered army squadron relics, the smarter savages had destroyed anyone who appeared they could offer resistance, while the second wave went to work on the women and children.

Of the 29 members in the small Mennonite convent, only two had managed to survive. Both children, a little girl named Dawn had crawled into a semi-cooled wood cook oven and 11 year old Will Otto in the underside of an overturned rain barrel which somehow had been overlooked during the carnage. Waiting motionless as the Indians chattered with triumph, the two emerged hours later as urine colored sun had become visible through the blurry plains of dust. Among two renegade savages dead in the dirt, every member of the traveling group had been murdered and what wasn't burnt of their camp was in tatters. Blood and gore as thick as glue coated the bodies and entrails were lying everywhere. They even killed the dog and hung it by his back legs beside an unborn baby ripped from its terrified mother's belly.

Horses stolen, along with all food and supplies, the two kids had waited aimlessly for hours around the camp in their blood covered clothes. Not knowing what to do or where to go, they discovered a mule that had broken loose and ran away when the screaming started and had wondered its way back to the scene. Scavenging birds of prey sensing a feast were already on hand and circled overhead in grim anticipation. Fearing the savages may return, the children threw a blanket caked with red stains from the carnage, over the animal's back, then set out to find water and began a journey to anywhere besides where they were.

Following a long afternoon of wandering aimlessly while the thirsty mule staggered into the twilight, shapes of honourably uniformed horsemen miraculously came into view. A horrible sight, dark blood on the children's clothes and faces had now dried to black in stark contrast to their dust covered white skin. Covered in ash from the cinders of the cook oven, parts of the girl's hair had been burned away and the boy had lost his shoes.

Ordering a halt, the regiment commander declared fires built immediately to bathe the youngsters and boil the stains from their cloths. The orphans were then wrapped in blankets and served roasted shoat, hard biscuits, fig jam and coffee. The poor mule was fed and watered as well.

Working his way up to position of foreman for the Union Pacific in later years, Otto had been part of the transcontinental railroad connect and moved along from stop to stop with the Hell on Wheels camps. Now a retired train robber, Otto and his group of associates had began by robbing banks, but trains had proven to be more profitable and offered less resistance from frightened passengers and crew who weren't the least bit interested in risking their lives for money that belonged to the railroad. Something he'd became all too familiar with during his years of unappreciated service to the company.

Each train consisted of engine and its tender annex, an express car, three to five passenger coaches, several boxcars (one of which on certain days held the payroll box guarded by two armed railroad employees) and a red caboose. Their attack would come just as the convoy began its long climb through a deep cut after pulling away from and well past its last water refilling station. With no choice but to slow to a crawl as the fire-fed steam locomotive struggled up the grade with thick black smoke billowing from its stack, the outlaws pushed their horses to close the gap as the train started its ascent, urging themselves close alongside the slowing cars.

Kerchiefs pulled below their eyes to hide their faces, emptying their pistols overhead with warning shots, one of the confederates would swing from his mount to the attached ladder of the engine platform and order the engineer to a halt. Following what seemed like an eternity to bring the giant convoy to a stop, the two payroll guards locked inside a boxcar would quickly disregard company orders not to open their door for anyone and surrendered without firing a shot from the threat of almost certain doom administered by four sticks of dynamite, blowing a hole in one end of the car and possibly blowing them out through the other.

Loading the contents of gold and currency from the smashed strongboxes in their saddlebags and riding off into the night, they had performed such daring robberies often during the 1880s. Getting their fill of being shot at and missed more times than they could count, not to mention getting hit a few times, they had accumulated enough cash to split up and each had gone their separate ways. Stricken with an acute infection some time later caused by contaminated water, no one wanted to be around a man dying of cholera, but one woman made it her priority to see after William and he had miraculously survived. The chubby fair skinned maiden's name was Melissa Chandler and it turned out… she was from Aurora.

Moving to the tiny town to settle down with his beloved, he quickly became a community favorite and his undiscovered past became a forgotten memory. Elected sheriff in an ironic turn of events in 1890, unfortunately things didn't go so well for his belovid. When the community was exposed to the spotted fever epidemic in 1891, she was stricken and died along with a great number of the town's population including Lynn's husband Bobby.

Holding up the steaming mug with a nod of good tidings, the cup had just grazed the sheriff's lips when his office door opened too quickly for any social call.

"Beggin' your pardon sheriff…" the man's voice grovelled with some shortness after seeing he'd interpreted their meal.

With his aggressive jaw, slightly hooked nose and intense gray eyes, "What now?" Otto growled rather impatiently through pursed lips. Clearly puzzled by the man's demeanour as she sat the untouched cup on the desk, Lynn looked up and rose to her feet.

"There's another one…" said the intruder.

"Another what?" Otto demanded!

"Flyin' Machine…" the man remarked, fear on his face, "We think they're lookin' for… him."

******

154

Chapter 18

Reptiles

1997

Reagan Stuart was without a doubt the love of Johnny Dale's life. As fresh and pure as the water that flowed from beneath the big mountain, full figured and blue eyed, she possessed the most beautiful flowing auburn hair and the loveliest smile to ever grace the lips of a woman. They'd met in high school quickly forming a friendship which grew into an irresistible relationship. Not your run of the mill drama filled gymnasium fling of vacillating lovers breaking up and making up more times than the average school boy could count on both fingers and toes, but a truly rare and heartfelt admiration between a young man and a young woman destined to last through the ages. The kind their elders bragged about when celebrating 40 plus years under the same roof without scars and resentment. The two played no games with each other, had no secrets, no sideline lovers. Everything seemed to line up in a row that couldn't have been straighter. Their families got along with no feuds, hell even the family dogs liked one another, not that Skeeter didn't get along with most anything that crossed his path. Marriage for the couple was inevitable. That's when it happened.

John was at work that day in the oil field. Part of a small repair crew doctoring an elderly pump jack when his grandpa's Dodge pickup came into view bumping across the field and pulling up alongside the rig. Johnny knew whatever it was that had brought papa Vickers out to his work sight wasn't going to be good but could never have been prepared for the tragic news he delivered.

Accepted to the University of North Texas, Fort Worth, where she and John planned to attend college together, Reagan was traveling home from a pre admittance visit when an out of control Chevy truck met her head on. The results were devastating. Intoxicated out of his mind yet again, the impaired driver of the fast moving killing machine fared no better, destroying not only his own life but several both old and young.

The viewing for the murderous alcoholic was clouded with shame from every angle and all in attendance held their breath when they realized who had walked into the room. Making his way to casket following a moment of nasty silence, John hocked and spit in the dead killer's face. The smallest penance for such a heinous crime in destroying the distraught intruder's future.

Abruptly swooped up by distraught family who knew not what else to do or say, ironically it was the mother of the killer who demanded for them to release the boy. Filled with anguish and tears she hugged and begged for his forgiveness for the reckless actions of her dead son.

Hearing the familiar roar of the cousin's 1946 Dodge truck, Johnny Dale sits outside the feed store, thinking of how life had been with her and of today's events, resting on the very same bench occupied earlier by the old codgers who alerted the reporter to the forgotten tale of his great grandpa's mysterious theft.

With no words he rises to meet Shannon the instant the pickup comes to a stop and crawling atop the five gallon can, once inside the cab, slams the door.

Noticing that his cousin is seemingly mad as a wet hen, "What's eatin' you cuz?" Shannon Ray asks.

Itching to share what he had heard, as they pull out of the store parking lot Johnny replied, "You ever remember hearin' a story 'bout our great grandpa Edward stealin' somethin' from a crash sight back when he was a kid?"

Thinking back, "I heard mama and Vickie talkin' one time," Shannon recalls like it's no big deal. "Said it was the reason pap use ta keep that ol' tool room locked in back'a the barn." Looking over at his cousin, wondering what all this is about, "Never thought much about it. Why?"

Staring forward with bitter determination for answers to the rest of the story, John rasps, "We'll find out soon as we get home."

"By suppressing the news? Withholding information?" Bonnie bellows as the conflict continues in the sheriff's office, "Ever hear of the First Amendment Mr. elected official? The Freedom of the press?" shaking the worse for ware copy once more, "This is information the public has every right to know!"

At his wits end, Shift warns, "I'm tellin' you... you're gettin' inta somethin' here you don't want to get involved with!"

"I am involved! And if I could buy tickets on it I'd bet half this whole damn town is involved!" Bonnie concludes as she heads for his office door, "Don't you worry...I'll figure this out all on my own." Not bothering to turn back as she exits, "Have a nice day... sheriff." slamming the door especially hard on her way out.

Shift's head falls forward in defeat. This woman was tough to beat. Whether he would allow himself to admit it or not, he admired her moxie and had no doubt she was a good sported soul despite her fit of momentary bravado. But that sure didn't make his job any easier and now he had a terrible headache. In more ways than one.

Storming out of the sheriff's office in a huff, three old codgers sit on a covered bench across the street, watching as the young reporter storms her way down the sidewalk and toward the parked black beauty belonging to her photographer.

"Little missy there's sure stirrin' up a lot a trouble." the first one says.

"Don't look like she's ready to quit neither." the second oldster adds.

The third man, old Clifton from the cafe, who rarely sits anywhere other than his unassigned seat at Kuff's front window, worriedly looks on but remains silent.

Decay from countless years of dry Texas heat has caused the wooden plank door of the small tool shed in the back of their grandpa's barn to become as fragile as peanut brittle. Having no curiosity toward the small room before, the cousins have laboured in this barn for years, passing by the forgotten door hundreds, if not thousands of times. Never giving a moment's thought to the contents it may hold. Until now.

The ancient hasp gives away as the boys pop the latch with a stray piece of flat steel found propped beside the '39 Ford. Forcing the door's rusty hinges, they cry out from lack of use. Peering in through the haze of disturbed dust, dark and dirty, there's never been any electric lights in this place. Outdated scythes and worn yard tools dating back decades are the only notable items inside other than a crude workbench.

Shannon holds a flashlight so the two can see. To the left, there's a lone shelf mounted high and out of reach with nothing on it except for a single wooden crate covered in a rotten piece of burlap. Silently, the boys look at one another with wonder before quickly dragging the bench across the tiny room to have something to stand on. Hoisting himself up, Johnny slowly pulls the rotten fabric away as mountains of dust fall to reveal an old wooden box marked *DUOBEL No2 HIGH EXPLOSIVES* in ancient letters. Yet another outdated padlock is attached to protect its contents. Exchanging glances once more in anticipation, John grabs hold of the box, hoists it off the shelf and to the floor.

Staggering into the motel room rented with her editor's charge card, Bonnie pitches her knapsack onto the bed. Flinging down beside it with fatigue, the book handed over for informative reading tumbles out of the bag and comes to rest touching her ear. Looking over, she scoops up the UFO work and purses her lips. Raising up and pitching it on the night table, she picks up the phone.

It's time to check in with the office and let her boss know she's on the right track.

At his editorial desk, Grail works to fix yet another mess created by a member of his team when pleasantly distracted as his secretary buzzes, "Chief, Miss Reynolds is on line two."

Whipping his glasses off with a smile, he snatches up the receiver and pushes the button. "My... my... if it isn't my roving reporter!"

"I don't know all that much yet," Bonnie begins, "but these folks know a lot more than they're letting on. I've also discovered there's an official government statement that claims the crash never happened."

"Don't I know!" he snaps on the other end of the line. "I've had another call this afternoon ordering me to shut you down and suppress your story."

Shooting straight up from her pillow, "Who called?" the reporter squeals, "The sheriff?"

"Never mind that now!" chuckling at the results of his new favorite columnist, he informs, "You may not know it, but whatever you're doing over there, you're rattling some chains and plucking some feathers!"

"But I ..." she began, only to be cut off again.

"Just stay on the story and get what you can get. Bring me some damning facts and I'll go with you all the way no matter who calls" then with a quick wisp of his head, the editor adds, "and Reynolds..."

"Yes?" She whispers.

"Proud of you girl!" before slamming down the phone.

Drawing a breath, Miss Reynolds realizes he's hung up and as much as she would like to find out more, she'd only be talking to an empty room. Who in Satan's fire could have possibly called him...about her? Frustrated beyond belief, she grabs a handful of her hair and tugs. The mystery of who was calling her employer now became overshadowed by the more intriguing enigma of why? What had began as a seemingly harmless assignment was now feeling a bit more sinister.

Resting on Johnny's worktable where most of the repairs pertaining to his motorcycle restoration take place, at just under two feet in length, the weight of the ancient dynamite box felt empty for the most part as it was hoisted up. Prying the vintage padlock, splinters and dust fly from the small wooden coffin which has held its secrets for so long. Wiping his hands across his shirt as if to clean and remove any perspiration from his excitement, Johnny slowly opens the lid. A very old yellowed newspaper lies folded atop a metallic object unlike anything either of the boys has ever seen.

Removing the crumbling newsprint, it turns out to be an original copy of the April 19, 1897 *Fort Worth Observer*, telling the story of the sky traveler who crashed into a windmill. Now in plain view, the gleaming object is oddly smooth like the freshly chromed bumper of an antique car but without the weight and with torn jagged sides as a result of the crash and explosion so long ago. Instantly the cousins realize that this is indeed what they were looking for. The stolen fragment from the extraterrestrial craft pilfered at the crash scene by their great grandpa Adam Edward Cochran 100 years ago. The very piece that people around these parts have been whispering and speculating about for generations. The piece some have even called their grandpa Vickers a liar over. Both boys secretly want to dance and cheer.

"Wh-what we gonna do with it J.D.?" Shannon Ray asks rather cautiously.

"I know exactly what we're gonna do…" Johnny says with determination as he closes the lid and swoops up the box, "We're goin' back inta town and find that pretty girl from the newspaper who kissed me today."

"Kissed you?" Shannon protests. Trailing behind his cousin as he makes his way to the truck, "You never said nothin' bout no girl a kissin' on you!"

Seated on the bucket, Shannon grabs a hold on the old explosives box as Johnny hands it over to him then trots around to the drivers side and slides behind the wheel of the pickup. Firing it up with a roar, they forget about Skeeter but as the truck begins to drive away he makes a mad dash and leaps over the tailgate.   Not to be left behind.

Bonnie heaves a heavy sigh as she lays her head atop several bunched up pillows on the bed. Closing her eyes, stretching her feet and wiggling her toes, "What a clusterfuck…" she breathes out. Longing to lay there and kick back, something tells her this just may not be the evening for relaxation. Self consciously, she knew she could stand to lose a good 10 pounds. Knew her belly wouldn't ever be as flat as she would have liked no matter how many meals she skipped or sit ups she did. One who didn't let anything stand in her way; she also knew what she wanted and how to get it. The thing she lacked was discipline. With big things like her career she was the most disciplined person she knew, however with little things… not so much.

Her mind kept reflecting on the confrontation with the sheriff and the tingling sensations that boy at the feed store made her feel. The encounter was totally innocuous and thrillingly erotic. "Damnit…" she mumbled. They were here to do a job and she intended to do it all the way but that didn't include lusting after the locals. She needed to focus.

So that boy's great grandfather snagged a piece of the alien spaceship right from the crash. "Haaa!" she unknowingly blurts to the empty room. "What a crock!" These folks must think she just fell off the turnip truck. But he was cute as hell, no doubt about that. Ok, enough about him dammit! She'd probably never see him again. And that sheriff, she knew there was something lacking with his story at the cafe, lowering his gaze to avoid her eyes when answering her questions. Handling the confrontation in his office a bit carelessly, she knew she should have acted more professional but dammit he had lied to her and that pissed her off. She was just doing her job. A follow up story to a freakin 100 year old legend. It isn't like she and Porter came over here with shovels to dig the little bastard up.

Rubbing her palms against her forehead, the fact that someone had called complaining of her presence here, that said wonders about the situation and made her feel a bit nervous. Maybe this alien legend was more serious than she'd first supposed? Looking over at the *Roswell* book, her boss had insisted it may make for "informative reading." She had so many ifs, whys and how's... maybe this book could answer some of her questions.

Lunch had been a disgusting disaster. The greasy sandwich unfit to eat on a day filled with leave home on the run for an unsuspecting assignment, Bonnie was starving and badly in need of a stiff drink. Thank goodness Aurora had one pizza joint that delivered; surely they offered a half decent salad. Picking up the phone and dialling Porters room she looks at the *Jay's Pizza* advertisement on the nightstand asking for his order and instructing him to be in her room in 20 minutes to eat. The boss is buying!

Finishing up with dinner a short 45 minutes later a knock came at Bonnie's door. "If it's those two lot lizards I saw earlier prowling around the parking lot," Porter warns, "whatever you do, don't let them in."

Passing the outdated RCA television, "Leave them to me." Bonnie reassures before fumbling to unlatch the stubborn safety chain. Opening the door, standing in the walkway before her, was one ghostly white obese prostitute and her rail thin black companion, both so ugly one would swear each had been repeatedly beaten with the preverbal ugly stick.

"Y'all like some company?" the oversize iguana began talking, "This is Nakishia and I'm Honey."

"Ahhh, thank you no, we're fine." the reporter dismisses then quick like a match flames when striking, she craves some much needed entertainment and leans a bit closer whispering, "It's not a good idea." nodding toward Porter, "See big sexy over there?" she teases. They both stare in his direction. "Romeo there is wanted by the law." Bonnie lies.

The pie face girl makes a pucker face while the dark one smiles.

Leaning even closer, as close as Bonnie dares without something jumping off the girls and onto her, she whispers, "Intent to commit forcible sodomy."

"Ewww!" pie face sneers.

"Woooo!" the other smiles, trying to step inside.

Quickly blocking her entry by thrusting an arm to the door frame, "Careful..." the reporter warns, "don't get too close." whispering again, "He's got a knife."

Having enough, the big girl clutches and begins tugging the dark one along to get away as the she injects with a wink, "We'll be in the parkin' lot if you change your mind!"

"You crazy fool." Porter scolds as Bonnie, laughing hysterically, closes the door, "What if they call the police?"

"Those reptiles??? Be serious. What could they possibly say?" Bonnie pretends to talk into a make believe receiver, "Hi, this is big Honey, you know the juicy queen-size prostitute who prowls the parking lot at the motel. I thought you'd like to know... there's a criminal sodomizer in room 112. Great big man with dark hair and funny glasses." Shaking her head, "I don't think so!"

"Not funny." Porter scolds as he rises to leave even though he can't help but laugh on his way out.

Showered and changing into a thin pastel sundress a short time later, propped on several pillows stacked on the headboard of her bed, Bonnie had had the good foresight to include a nearly full bottle of Captain Morgan in her knapsack and was on her third rum and Coke thanks to some much needed ice and Diet Cokes from the motel vending machine. Hunkered down to begin the book's account of what happened one state over in New Mexico during that fateful summer of 1947, the story soon became amazingly clear. Leaning back and getting comfy,   she begins to read...

******

Chapter 19

Moaning

1947

Following the Great Airship Mystery of 1896-97, sightings and descriptions of curious flying craft with strange lights continued well into the 20th century and beyond. With the development of early 1900s hot air balloons, floating dirigibles and primitive airplanes, flying objects were becoming more common in the sky, but any extensive media coverage toward unexplained hovering craft became overshadowed by the conflict of World War I.

In the 1920s and 30s there were many reports of "ghostly aircraft" which no one seemed to be able to identify passing over military installations. There was a definite strangeness to the reports of circling craft which emitted powerful multicolored lights, but at the time no real way to thoroughly track their movement. That all changed with the advent of radar in the early '40s. Following a growing epidemic of "Unidentified Flying Objects" sightings after World War II, most were considered only second hand news in local papers gaining little or no notoriety. Then one particular headline of a U.F.O. sighting changed things...forever.

The term "Flying Saucer" didn't exist in the American vocabulary until 1947. It began with a report from Deputy Federal Marshal Kenneth Arnold, a private pilot of the Idaho Search and Rescue Mercy Flyers. On June 24th, Arnold had joined a search mission in the Cascade Mountains of Washington State. At 2 p.m., flying at an altitude of 9,200 feet, he witnessed a *"tremendously bright flash"* reflected off his aircraft alerting him to nine bright silver discs flying in formation.

Traveling at the unprecedented speed of 1,700 miles per hour, three times the speed of sound, this was a time in history when no aircraft constructed by human hands could possibly achieve speeds anywhere close to that. In a newspaper interview of his encounter with the *East Oregonian*, Arnold described, that they *"flew like saucers skipping across the water."* Picked up by the Associated Press, they called the discs, *"saucer-like objects"* from which the term "Flying Saucer" was born and became permanently embedded as an integral part of our language. With this highly publicized sighting, the incident ignited a wave of widespread media attention causing the public to take the subject of flying craft from other worlds much more seriously.

Then came the Roswell crash.

Falling out of the sky during a lightning storm, as if sent by heaven above, no other downed flying saucer story has commanded such worldwide attention to the UFO community. It has become the most well documented extraterrestrial case in the world and it all began on the evening of July 4th, 1947.

Following several reports of a mysterious silver spaceship sighted over New Mexico on Wednesday July 3rd, shortly before bedtime the next day, Corporal E.L. Piles was the first to see the object race across the sky and plummet down. The craft *"had an orange glow around it with what appeared to be a halo toward the front and was bright enough to be seen 30-40 miles away."*

Catholic nuns Mary Bernadette and Sister Capistrano of Roswell's St. Mary's Hospital, making their nightly rounds, also saw the brilliant light plunge to earth. Believing it to be a disabled aircraft of some kind, they recorded the event in their logbook shortly after 11pm.

Seeking a quiet getaway for the summer holiday, nearby residents James Ragsdale and Trudy Truelove were camping in the desert landscape on the Plains of San Augustine when *"a bright blue-grey object"* roared over their campsite and slammed to the ground roughly a mile away. All the while, Military technicians at the Roswell Air Base and White Sands were closely monitoring the *"unidentified flying object"* zig zagging across southern New

Mexico on radar. At 11:20 p.m. the object, which defied the laws of any conventional aircraft, began acting erratically. It then seemed to explode into a *"fire burst"* at 11:27 and disappeared from their screen shortly afterward. With no way to pinpoint an exact location, but knowing the object was down somewhere north of Roswell, a comprehensive search was scheduled for dawn.

Dr. W.C. Holden along with a small group of archaeology students from Texas Tech were first to discover the crash sight. Performing excavations in the nearby area, they had watched the "strange blue-white object" fall to earth from their campsite the night before and set out before sunrise to search for it. What they found, just off of Pine Ridge Road, was more than they could have ever bargained for.

"The craft looked like a crushed dishpan around 30 ft. long with a scalloped bat-like wing." one of the party recalled. *"Slamming into the ground at a thirty degree angle, there was a large hole in its left side with debris*

scattered all around. Three small humanoid bodies were visible outside the wrecked fuselage, each with ashy gray skin, pear shaped heads and no hair. They had strange recessed slanted eyes and wore thin silver metallic clothing." Miraculously, one had survived the impact and moved to a small cliff, sitting upright with a serene look upon his face. A woman in Holden's team stated, *"The poor thing had been injured in the crash. Its blood was black as tar and stained its silver uniform. The survivor's bluish grey skin appeared to be similar to that of an iguana. With only a small slit for a mouth, tiny apertures in the place of ears and a vague nose, it couldn't have weighed more than 50 pounds."*

Minutes later Ragsdale and Truelove arrived by Jeep from their campground and got out to get a good look at what had happened. Frightened, Trudy insisted they *"get the hell out of here"* just as the wail of approaching sirens and thunder of heavy trucks became unmistakable. Retreating to a secluded spot, they witnessed a 1947 Ford filled with Army M.P.'s under the command of Major Edwin Easley led a convoy of military vehicles to surround the area and take control of the situation.

The archaeologists were abruptly rounded up, ordered to face away from the crash and surrender their identification before being loaded into military vehicles and taken to the army base for interrogation. As the scene was being thoroughly photographed, Ragsdale and Truelove moved further back to keep out of sight and then quietly slipped away before being noticed.

Roswell fire fighter Dan Dwyer was one of the first responders to an emergency call of a downed aircraft. The fire department wasn't allowed directly on the scene by Air Force officials but Dwyer and his crew clearly saw several body bags being loaded into a retired ambulance and a small distressed being about the size of a 10 year old child. All in attendance witnessed the hairless foreign creature being escorted to a military vehicle and driven away. The responders had no doubt that these beings were not human.

One of the guards at the crash site, Melvin E. Brown, was ordered to *"climb into that ambulance and make sure no one touched anything"* but to *"leave the body bags alone"* The moment he was alone, he couldn't resist observing that *"the bodies were smaller than humans with large heads and leathery skin like that of a lizard,"* Brown then rode with the bodies back to the Air Base hospital.

Sergeant Frank Kaufman was on duty the same night base radar tracked the UFO and was part of the detail dispatched to locate the crash. Forming a semicircle around the craft, he recalled, *"it was greyish white with a soft light coming from cell like structures covering the bottom of the craft and an orange aura from inside where a seam had split open. A large truck with a crane was rigged up by the guys from the Air Base motor pool to lift the craft and load it onto a flatbed truck."* It was then put on a train and shipped to Muroc Air Base in California for analysis.

Civilian contractor Roy Musser, painting in the rear section of the Roswell Air Base Hospital around noon the same day, witnessed a *"small creature, very slender and child like, walk into the rear entrance under military escort."* Murcer was told to get out immediately and warned *"never to mention what he had seen or he and his family would be in jeopardy."*

New Mexico Lieutenant Governor Joseph Montoya also saw the creature. Montoya was flirting with several of the hospital's nurses while awaiting a flight back to Albuquerque when the alien made its entrance. Greatly upset when he saw the survivor, he described to his family, *"It was small with a big head and larger than normal eyes and was moaning mournfully. Sitting with its knees up, they were so skinny that he didn't look human."* Montoya was so shaken he left the base, went to the home of a friend and got intoxicated, then caught a flight home the following day.

Young Glenn Dennis working as a mortician at Roswell's Ballard Funeral Home began receiving phone calls around 1:30 p.m. from the Air Base Mortuary office. He was inquiring as to *"the availability of hermetically sealed child sized caskets"* as well as *"what type of cosmetology preservatives wouldn't destroy the composition of bodies that had been lying out in the elements."* In charge of ambulance service for RAAF, later the same day Dennis returned an injured airman to the base. At the emergency room entrance he noticed three old box-type field ambulances parked near the ramp with the rear doors open and fragments of shiny material inside. Inside the hospital he saw nurse Naome Self who hysterically hissed, *"Glenn! How did you get in here? You're going to get into big trouble! Get out as fast as you can!"* But before he could, Glenn was spotted and threatened by red-headed Captain Joe Kittinger who called him a son of a bitch and told him if he told anyone anything he may have seen or heard, *"somebody will be picking your bones out of the sand!"* Marching the mortician back to his ambulance, they demanded for him to leave and watched until he was out of sight.

Five p.m. and things were rolling, Hangar 84 at the air base was cleared out to store a long wooden crate containing the bodies from the crash. Sealed for transport, it was placed in the center of the building and illuminated by a spotlight. Melvin Brown, who'd ridden with the bodies to the facility, was a member of the guard detail with strict orders to shoot anyone who approached without authority.

Under the cover of darkness at around 2 a.m. and the supervision of Steve Mackenzie, (one of the officers that had been tracking the object or radar) the hangar light was turned off and using maximum security conditions with only flashlights to see, the crate was loaded onto an Army C-54 for flight.

W.O. "Pappy" Henderson, pilot in command of that flight with the 1st Air Transport unit, later remarked, "*A concerted TOP SECRET effort was used to create diversions along the flight, intended to cover our trail just in case anyone tried to follow.*" The plane delivered the crate to Andrews Air Force Base in Washington where its contents were inspected by several high ranking officials including then Army Chief of Staff Dwight D. Eisenhower. It was then taken onto Wright-Patterson Airfield in Dayton Ohio.

Back in Roswell, the Army was working overtime to feverishly try and prevent any news of the day's events from spreading. Every member of both local police and fire departments who had responded to the early morning scene, including Don Dwyer, were sought out and interrogated in their homes.

Dwyer's daughter recalled that her father, "*arrived home after his shift and could barely contain himself.*" gathering the family to tell what he'd witnessed, "*We stood there, not believing what we were seeing. A crashed flying saucer with one crew member still alive and walking around. His face looked like the Child of the Earth insect and he communicated to us in our heads. Without saying a word, we all heard the same thing. That it was sad over the loss of his comrades and that no one could help him but they were not there to hurt us.*" Soon after this confession the Military arrived at their home and stormed inside. "*There were four of them, armed with rifles.*" Dwyer's daughter claimed the officer in charge sat the entire family down yelling at her father, "*Forget what you may have seen or heard and if you ever talk about it we will kill you and take your bodies out into the desert where no one will ever find you!*" Then they left.

******

Chapter 20

Trophy

1997

His bullhide boots a tad more dusty than normal; Denny Chote has his feet propped in the seat of a chair under the patio section of the local bar. Unable to make his regular evening rounds for obvious reasons, the sheriff had invited him for a drink and to discuss the day's trying events. Sitting out front under the decks covered awning, guzzling a much needed tall cold brew, Denny suggests, "Don't ya think you're overreactin' just a little?"

"Naw...not this time." Shift says almost mechanically. Deeply worried he went on, "That girls gonna bring the wrath'a God down on this town with her nosing around and us along with it." then staring blankly into the game warden's face, "What if she finds out? Then what do we do?"

"Sheriff... you copy?" Shift's handheld radio beeps.

Ignoring the device he repeats himself "What-do-we-do?" as if Denny hadn't heard. Turning his attention to the call with the push of a button, "Go for sheriff."

"Sheriff," an older lady's voice comes over the tiny speaker, "Tom Hardy called. Said that Jackie Jones' cows were in the road again and that he's outta town at a car auction... come back."

Snarling with a shake of the head, "Will this day never end?" Shift grumbles with a haggard look. Pushing the mike he replies, "10-4... Call Clint Dailey; tell him to bring Klayton and R.J. along. Have them meet me out there..." concluding heavily, "I'm on my way."

"10-4" the voice answers.

Looking over at his friend with a hopeful grin, "Feel like playing cowboy?"

"Nope!" the game warden answers confidently. "Not tonight!" he adds with a smirk and a chuckle.

"Fine then..." the sheriff puffs. Stuffing the cash he'd pulled out for the bill back in his pocket, "...you pay the tab." Putting on his Stetson and throwing the last of his beer back in his throat Andrew pulls at his jeans and heads for the parking lot. Left to sip his brew in peace, the game warden's moment of calm is short lived. As the sheriff's cruiser pulls away from the bar in one direction, the Cochran boy's noisy ass truck races by in the other. "Damn them trouble makin' bastards!" Chote grumbles with a tight jaw.

Following sight of the old pickup because he just can't help himself but look, its brake lights flash on as it slows down the street. Coming to a halt with a squeak of its brakes, the vehicle turns into the parking lot of the Aurora motel. An odd place for those two to be heading, especially this time of the evening, Denny notices as he suddenly makes the connection and mutters, "Holy... Cats..."

Turning away as if the problem would simply go away on its own, checking out the tall waitress wearing Daisy Dukes as she bends to wipe a neighbouring table, "Here we go..." he growls chugging the last of his beer with a long deep gulp. Slamming the mug down hard enough on the wooden table for the waitress to pause with caution, he rises from the comfortable spot, tips his hat to her as an apology and tugs at his paints to pull them up a notch before starting out on foot in the direction of the motel.

"*Travelers*", the fifteenth episode of the fifth season of *The X-Files* with guest star Darren McGavin, a.k.a. *Kolchak: The Night Stalker*, plays quietly in the background on the outdated motel television set, but our young reporter pays no attention. Reading of armed soldiers threatening dozens of citizens with death if they breathed a word of what they had seen or heard concerning the Roswell crash, our reporter has discovered a startling account of government corruption and cover up concerning an actual crashed flying saucer in July, 1947.

BAM-BAM-BAM!

Bonnie nearly jumps out of her skin when interrupted by a heavy handed knock at her room's door. Looking at the night table clock it projects a digital red 7:40 p.m. "Not those reptiles again?" she mumbles. No, she'd been out for ice and saw no sign of them. If not though, who would possibly be knocking at her door in a town where she knew no one? Sliding off the bed and adjusting her sundress, the last thing she wanted was for a stray boob to be hanging out for some stranger to see. Easing to the door half dressed and barefoot, she wearily peeps through the peephole.

Surprised but relieved to see a familiar face standing on the other side, it's the handsome young man she'd kissed only a few hours before. Unlocking the door and trying to open it, she fusses and fumbles with the temperamental night chain which of course now seems to be hopelessly stuck. Refusing to slide out of the track after several attempts of picking and pulling, she's had it with the attempt and jerks the door open ripping the hasp from the wall.

The instant the door flies opens, a multicolored dog races in the room causing Bonnie to start with a yelp. Her eyes wide, they follow sight of the four legged intruder as it jumps on her bed, tail wagging like a flag in the wind.

Turning back to the boy outside, "John! What on earth are you doing here?" she ruffles. Another scrawny boy of about the same age stands on her doorstep, just as stinkin' cute as the other but with dark wavy hair; her attention goes to a bulky old wooden box he's holding.

Not the least bit lost for words this time, Johnny hands over the dusty 100 year old newspaper and looks her straight in the face with a decisive, "To prove my granddaddy ain't no liar."

Accepting the vintage newsprint, Bonnie instantly recognizes its significance. A vintage original copy of the 1897 *Fort Worth Observer* highlighting the story of the Aurora crash, one of two related articles she had made reference copies from before leaving the office. The very news story that has caused her to become involved in all this mess. Staring at the dusty box for only a moment, realizing that this is no social call, her brain recollects the old man's account of a fragment from the crash being stolen by this boy's great grandfather. "Oh-My-God..." she whispers in astonishment.

Poking her head outside the doorway to make sure no one is watching, she reaches and grabs Johnny once again by the top button of his cut off flannel shirt. "Get in here!" she quickly herds the boys into her room and slams the door. Locking the handle and reaching for the safety chain, which now broken and dangling isn't going to do anybody any good, she frowns and flings it to the side. Spinning to eye the cousins with her wrist covering her mouth, puffing out an exasperated breath, she tries hard to comprehend what may be inside the box. Was it possible? A piece of… it?

"Holy... Shit." Bonnie mutters, pointing at the crate as if it indeed was filled with ancient and unstable dynamite ready to explode in front of her. Blood pounding in her ears and head, "That can't be …?" she asks in a low almost frightened voice.

With all the confidence in the world, Johnny begins, "That old man at the feed store told you he'd heard my great grandpa runoff with a piece'a that crashed vehicle back in the 1800s. I did remember my grandpa sayin' somethin' like that, but it'd been so long I'd plum forgot." Motioning for Shannon to slide back the still half full pizza box left behind by the photographer and sit the crate down, "That is till that crotchety ol' buzzard called my grandpa a liar and I started thinkin' about it." he continues walking over to the box and reaching for the lid, "We went home an' found this locked in an old shed. Ain't been opened for years an I'm showin' it to ya cause my grandpa's the finest man I've ever known and he damn sure ain't no liar." With Skeeter now off the bed and standing happily by Bonnie's side, the boy opens the lid.

The reporter's mouth falls open in astonishment at the sight of the silver spaceship fragment delivered to her door by the young men. Afraid to get too close but taking a cautious step forward and leaning over to have a closer look at the strange object, "WOW…" she whispers, "It-is-true…"

Always the prankster and seeing the perfect opportunity for a gag, Shannon Ray moves quietly behind the reporter and shouts a spooky, "Woo-Woo-Woo-Woo…" in imitation of a spacecraft powering up to lift off.

Causing Bonnie to yelp for a second time in as many minutes, she spins and delivers a bold slap to Shannon's face. "Asshole!" the reporter brazenly wails. Skeeter as if almost seconding her displeasure, lets out a growl.

Casting a nasty stink-eye at Johnny who's trying desperately not to snicker, "Who the fuck is this clown?" she hisses.

"My cousin Shannon Ray." John dismisses with a wave, "Fancies himself a jokester." still trying not to break into laughter, "Pay him no mind." Her back turned, a proud Shannon gives his cousin a quick wink of triumph.

Backing away and pointing firmly toward the bed, "Sit down you little chicken shit!" the girl demands of the dark haired cousin. Reaching for the phone and pounding several numbers, "I'll kick your lanky little ass... funny boy!" she threatens the joker. Skeeter shows his teeth and growls at his master, as if now totally on the girl's side. "Porter!" she shrieks into the receiver a bit louder than meaning, "Get over here right now! And bring your camera!" Listening to the reaction on the other end, she roars, "Both of them!"

Regardless of the fact that Johnny had come to show her the newly discovered piece, he'd gotten off his chest what he needed to say and could now barely keep his eyes off the young reporter. She too he thought was simply delicious. Knowing no boundaries, the instant Bonnie is off the phone, Shannon asks the reporter in a whiney tone, "We ain't had no time for supper, mind if I have some'a that pizza?"

A short time later the door to the reporter's room opens as the mischievous pair exit and begin briskly across the parking lot with the box. Followed faithfully by their dog, just as they reach the old Dodge, Denny Chote steps out from behind the other side. "Howdy boys..." he draws daringly, arms folded. Then looking down at their companion acknowledges, "...Skeeter." to the curt reply of a woof.

Startled himself now the jokes on Shannon. As if confronting an unwanted ghost, he blurts, "H-hey D-D-Denny," stumbling on, "W-wha-what you doin' over here?"

"Might ask you the same thing?" he replies sceptically with a nod to the bulky load Shannon's holding, "What's in the box?"

"Nothin'!" the two reply almost in unison. Both turning a lovely pale shade of green.

"Y'all headin' out to blow up somethin'?" he asks in reference to the *Duobel High Explosives* box.

"OH NO DENNY!! WE'D NEVER..." Shannon cries.

Half smiling at the comedy of it all, the game warden bends closer to the boys with a low growl, "Wouldn' happen to be ol' Adam Edward's trophy... would it?"

As his mouth falls open Shannon Ray gasps, "How'd you..." before John elbows him with a jab in his ribs to silence.

"I figured as much." Denny admonishes with a sigh, "Showed it to that little reporter filly, diddn' ya?" Saying nothing and trying their best to avoid eye contact, the boy's actions speak louder than words. Painting a clear picture for Denny, he takes a deep breath and wishes he had another drink. Jerking a thumb toward the back of the old truck, the game warden grimaces, "Get in!"

Petrified at this point, Shannon stutters, "Wh-where we goin'?" whimpering on, "Ain't nowheres fer us ta sit since we lost our timber."

Smacking him harder this time, Johnny groans, "Don't you *EVER* know when ta shut up?"

Pursing his lips to an ugly frown, Denny has no choice at the moment but to ignore the comment, simply narrowing his eyes and repeating, "Get in!"

Helping the dog up and over the tailgate, as the boys crawl in the back of their truck handing the box from one to another and sitting down with their backs propped against the cab, Denny then slides into the driver's seat of the multicolored jalopy. Straining his eyes in the darkness to make out the dashboard, trying to figure out how to start the damn thing, the game warden grumbles amusingly, "Hmmm, never thought I'd be caught doin' this."

Pushing the old fashioned starter button after a flip of the switch, the old rig roars to life. Grinding the gears a time or two before finding first, Denny puts on his sun shades regardless of the fact that it's night. A wasted effort to try and avoid humiliation. Bumping slowly across the parking lot with his hat pulled low, the game warden recognizes a familiar unmarked black government car as it pulls into the rear of the motel from the street with its headlights off. With the box and its contraband safely nestled between the boys, thankful to be incognito, Denny rolls on.

******

Chapter 21

Lynn

1897

The moon was full and bright and on the far side of town another orb was glowing like a brushfire creeping along at about five to ten miles an hour. Hovering brightly in the night sky, it headed toward Aurora with a bright beam of light focused toward the ground. Spectators huddled in bunches holding lamps and torches to light the street.

From the boardwalks citizens watched the floating vessel from chairs with their feet propped on hitch posts. One grizzled oldster with a dusty beard eyed the skies from a rickety rocking chair. A palomino tied to a hitch rail danced and blew nervously as the craft came closer. Still there remained a sense of calm until one bonnet covered lady, known affectionately throughout the community as aunt Lovie, strolled out of a shop. Completely unaware of what was happening outside, looking up to see what everyone was staring at, she saw the object soaring overhead with the grace of an eagle and let out a shrill scream.

"Shut her up!" someone hollered, but the silence was broken. Making nary a sound heard by human ears, two dogs so far silent began to yammer as if something irritated their senses while brilliant bluish cones of light flooded over the tops of buildings at the end of the street.

"Look there…" someone tapped the sheriff on the shoulder as he stood in the street staring at the airship. Turning his head to follow the man's finger, there was another. The sight of not just one but two airborne spacecraft would be beyond belief if it weren't for the unprecedented happenings of the morning.

"Lookin' fer em, ain't they sheriff?" another man in the crowd said in hushed tones.

"Maybe so…" Otto growled, "Lord help us if they are." A near blinding beam found the crowd and stopped. Warming their faces like rays of the summer sun in contrast to the cool April night air, it cast hard silhouettes of their bodies on the dirt at their feet. Emanating only the faintest sound, the silver ship remained motionless for a time as if examining the onlookers before continuing on seemingly uninterested in the people of the small dusty town. Staring upward to observe its smooth metal bottom, folks held their breath as it passed directly over. The faint humming cast by the mysterious hovering object was the only sound around until the all too familiar click of a rifle hammer being pulled back was heard.

Triggered by creeping fear of the unknown, one of the onlookers had raised his Henry repeater and was ready to fire. "Idiot!" the sheriff scolded with a harsh whisper. Slapping the barrel toward the ground, he growled, "You wanna get us all killed? If they can fly, it's a pretty good guess they can shoot too!" Looking at the surrounding frightened faces, he continued with words as comforting at possible, "For heaven's sake folks, there's no comeuppance upon none of us! Everthin's gonna be fine, so long as we don't panic."

Passing over the lower end of town, the craft's beams of illumination rained down on the burned out remains of Auroras charred buildings. Fear-stricken citizens now on edge, cautiously made their way to the safety of covered boardwalks or looked out from inside structures through dirty windows while others stood their ground to follow the crafts movement.

Understanding now the magnitude of what had fallen from the sky and crashed in their small town. It had become evident to all; the creature they had buried today was indeed a traveler from another planet... another world. Somewhere else, that was clear and now it was quite obvious his cohorts were looking for their lost companion. The question that came was - If they made it through the night and these brilliant floating machines moved on, would they be back? Would there be... others?

Low muttering voices from the crowd began as the silver craft circled the battered remains of the water tower. The beam transfixed on the scene illuminating it clearly in the pitch black. If they hadn't know better one would have thought the destruction an act of sabotage caused by several sticks of dynamite or a good size bottle of nitro-glycerine.

"Keep goin'. Keep... goin'..." Otto muttered with worry, "What happened to your friend wouldn' none'a our doin'." regarding the early morning crash.

Examining the scene for a moment, what seemed like an hour to the on looking crowd, the beam suddenly lifted and the craft passed in front of the moon and into the distance, vanishing into the night sky as quickly as it had appeared. Had they found what they were looking for? An explanation for their missing comrade perhaps?

"Think they'll come back?" someone asked.

"Couldn' tell ya." Otto replied, his voice filled with a distant ring that made him sound far away.

With the rifle still in his grasp the foolish resident who may have put everyone in peril hacked, "Should'a shot em when I had the chance." as the crowd begins to disperse.

The reformed Texas lawman shook his head, turned and started back to his office for the now cold meal so thoughtfully prepared for him by his beloved. Lynn. At least the company waiting for him would be warm and inviting and this incredibly stressful day in the spring of 1897 was at a close. Maybe now everyone could simply forget it ever happened.

Then again... maybe not.

******

Chapter 22

Shoot em

1997

Stubborn cows take their time, moving slowly as several men hold swinging lanterns in an effort to hasten them along. Sheriff Shift of Wise County along with his buddies work patiently with the escaped heifers to herd them back through the section of downed fence and back where they belong.

As the distinct roar of a fast engine and a pair of vintage headlamps come into view, Shift wonders why the Cochran boys are out this time of night in a section of the county opposite from where they live. When old Vicker's truck pulls up to the scene he can't help but smile with contempt as Denny opens the driver's door and steps out.

"Well… ain't this one for the record books?" he goads the game warden for driving around in the very vehicle he despises so much. Flashing a bewildered look toward the trio as the boys crawl out of the back, "Come'ta help?" he quips. The boys look down in silence as Denny folds his arms. "Naw…" Shift dismisses sadly, "I diddn' think so."

Leading the sheriff toward the back of the pickup, "Why do I get the feelin' this is about to become unpleasant?" Shift asks as Denny lowers the tailgate to expose the wooden crate. "Damn, y'all headed out to blow somethin' up?" he jokes of the box marked *HIGH EXPLOSIVE* as Denny reaches forward and flips open its lid. Jerking his body back as if a poisonous snake were inside and his head toward sight of the cousins with a vengeful screech, **"Have you two dipshits lost your fuckin' minds?** Out here ridin' this thing around!" His face filled with terror of consequence, Shift slams the lid and continues, "You have any idea how dangerous that is?" Skeeter barks out in full agreement.

Worried and shaken with the sudden turn of events, the boys stare toward the ground to avoid eye contact. In a low monotone voice Denny looks to them and scowls, "Tell him." Sometimes the best thing is silence. The boys say nothing. With no confession the sheriff anxiously looks to his friend for answers. "Showed it to that girl from Gainesville." Denny groans.

"YOU DID NOT!" the lawman screams to the cousins. Thrashing around like a shark ready to strike, dancing in circles and out of his mind, "Goddammit to hell almighty!" he cries pointing to the box, "Here I take up for you two trouble-makin' brats and you go and do THIS?"

Praying for a miracle on the off chance that he misunderstood, he interrogates the cousins, "You-did-not-show...THAT...to that feline reporter?"

Already knowing the answer, with no response he yells, "Do you have any idea the amount a damage you've done?" then snapping his gaze to his friend, orders, "Denny... shoot em!"

The game warden cracks a genuine smile and lowers his hand to his weapon with no intention to draw. Cowering in fear, both boy's knees buckle at the command to execute and they hit the ground. Raising their hands toward heaven for help Johnny spits, "This is been a secret for way too long. We only wanted to prove our grandpa weren't no liar."

In fear of never seeing his sexy young girlfriend again, Shannon Ray pipes up excitedly, "Yeah Sheriff, you know what they say… The truth will set you free." A failed attempt to be humorous.

"Truth!" the sheriff retorts un-amused, "The truth can get us all killed!"

"There's more…" Denny adds dryly.

Craning his neck until it hurts, "Jesus freakin Christ!" the sheriff implores, "Don't know if I can stand much more tonight."

In a deep throaty voice, Denny informs, "Our 'friend' from the bureau…"

"Not that son of a bitch!" Shift spits venomously.

Nodding to the affirmative "Saw him pullin' into the motel lot where the girls stayin' as we was pullin' out." Denny confirms.

Shaking a hysterical finger toward the dynamite box, "With THAT in back of the truck?" the sheriff snaps, "Holy-shit!" Pacing, standing, then pacing some more, the lawman thinks hard as he tries to regain his composure and come up with their next move. Looking to the game warden he says calmly, "Watchin' the reporter…" Not a question but a factual statement explaining the agent's sudden and unwanted appearance.

"Mmmm-hmmm…" Denny nods.

Wondering whether or not the simplest plan of action would be to simply shoot himself at this point, Shift professes, "They think she may be gettin' close. Well by god…she wanted a story." then giving the two troublemakers his best evil eye, "Thanks ta you two pecker woods she sure as hell got one."

Looking back at Denny, he takes a deep breath releasing an airy, "Ain't but one thing left to do now… let's go."

"That was the coolest thing I've ever seen in my whole life!" Porter says sitting on the corner of Bonnie's bed with the grin of a boy on Christmas morning who's just received the gift he's always wanted. "You know Grail would be climbing his office walls now if he knew what we saw." regaling with humour, "Yelling, stamping his feet, breaking windows, he'd probably shoot himself by midnight if he thought a story like this might miss the morning edition."

"You just do as I say!" Bonnie instructs her assistant with no room for doubt. Yesterday she would have labelled all this as crazy. The world had changed now, her world at least. No one believes in things that haven't touched them in personal ways. People tend to stick with what they know and journey down life's road with the comfortable and familiar. Bonnie was one of those for the most part. She had seen the mundane, the bizarre and the everyday happenings of life but today in the little town of Aurora Texas she had seen an actual fragment from an extraterrestrial spaceship.

"Take that film back to the office and develop it. I don't care if it takes you all freakin night." she demands shaking the exposed roll just emptied from his camera and raising her voice an octave to further emphasize her wishes. "Get the prints from it dry and hide them someplace safe." then adding, "and whatever you do… don't show them to anyone! Got it?"

"Got it!" he confirms sharply, "What about…"

"Me?" Bonnie answers, knowing his next question. "I'll be just fine. Now you GO and don't worry!"

The corrupt federal onlookers in the far corner of the parking lot are keeping a watchful eye on Miss Reynolds. "That's her." Ralph, the town snitch confirms as the reporter sticks her head out to see if anyone is looking. From the secluded position they watch patiently as Porter leaves the room and walks to his car.

"Who's that?" the agent asks.

"Her assistant." the rat squeaks with a passive gesture.

"Wonder where he's going this time of night?" Travers muses.

"Fat ass, out for more comic books... pizza maybe, who knows? She's the one we need to keep an eye on."

Propped again on her pillows now that the photographer was safely on his way back to Gainesville, he possessed all the evidence she needed to verify what is sure to be an award winning story. More than anxious to get back to the second half of her editor's book, after what she'd seen tonight she would never doubt the enigma of flying saucers ever again. It's one thing to hear stories and legends of UFOs, quite another to see pieces of one in person from an innocent young man who had nothing else to gain other than set the record straight. Her mind boggled.

In the first half of the book she had learned that what the army had taken possession of in the desert on July 5th 1947 was very much like what she had just seen, beyond comprehension. An aircraft constructed by beings from another planet and capable of flying some millions of miles through space, propelled by a force as yet unknown.

Secrets revealed from the craft ultimately led to the development of such items as lasers, integrated circuitry, fiber-optics, particle-beams, night vision technology, bullet-proof Kevlar and multiple items useful in the development of space related defence systems. All this and more harvested and developed from advanced technology found in the wreckage of the crash in Roswell.

The survivors fate, who came to be known as EBE (extraterrestrial biological entity) was considered an unsolved mystery until thankfully a top secret transcript from a CIA UFO caretaker to President Reagan was leaked to the public.

The Presidential document stemming from a March 1981 briefing verified *"that the living alien from the Roswell crash turned out to have experienced only minor injuries and was sent to Sandia Labs at Los Alamos where a special housing unit was set up for him."* It went on to explain that, *"He lived there until he died of an unexplained illness on June 18, 1952."* During his time there he related that he was from *"the Zeta Reticuli star system, approximately 40 light years from earth"* and *"supplied the government with a great deal of technical information."*

But that was only half of the story.

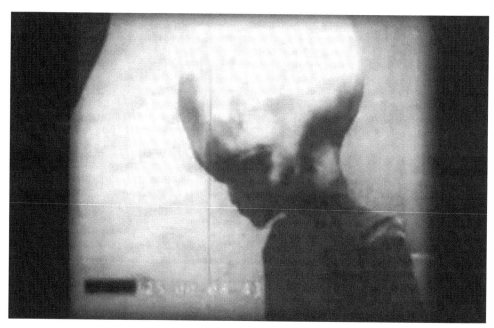

******

Chapter 23

Horseback

1947

Following the extraordinary lengths the military had taken to keep the crash under wraps, Washington officials at the time believed maybe, just maybe, the incident could remain a government secret. If it hadn't been for the actions of a scruffy old sheep farmer with scuffed up boots, the true story of the July 4th crash may have never reached the American public.

The second half of the Roswell story went something like this.

Sheep rancher Mac Brazel climbed into his old farm truck to make the nearly 100 mile drive from Corona into Roswell to inform Chaves County Sheriff George Wilcox of the strange find he had made on the Foster Ranch. Hearing an odd explosion during a severe lightning storm shortly before midnight on July 4th, Brazel and a neighbour had set out at sun up the next morning to investigate. On horseback, they discovered that *something had crashed on his property, making a huge mess and littering his south pasture with metallic debris so dense the sheep refused to cross the area.*

Not considering it a priority at the moment, he continued his daily chores until the next morning when talk of flying saucer reports in the area drew his attention. It was then he decided it may be best to gather a few pieces of the wreckage and report it. A decision he would regret until his death.

Showing Wilcox some of the strange pieces, the sheriff too had heard details of the commotion the day before and thought it best to notify Roswell Army Base. Intelligence officer Major Jesse Marcel of the 509th Bomb Group took the call. One that would change the course of his life.

Hearing Brazel's story, the Major advised the rancher to sit tight. Believing there a possible connection to the reported UFO crash, he would be on his way as soon as possible. Accompanied by Senior Intelligence Agent Captain Sheridan Cavitt, they escorted Brazel from the sheriff's office back to his ranch. Arriving at Brazel's ranch after dark, they all bedded down for the night, had a meal consisting of cold beans and waited for daylight to investigate.

The scene of whatever had taken place was enormous. It appeared to Marcel and the others as if *"some large object had exploded in the air above the ground then slammed down on the property shattering massive pieces of its construction. Gouging up the dirt as it moved, it then somehow lifted back up again and continued on to the southwest."*

The officers spent the day examining the three-quarters of a mile long partially burnt debris field. Picking up piles of wreckage, they collected mounds of *"strange foil like material that couldn't be cut or burnt, plastic looking I-beams with indecipherable two-color markings and a black material resembling bakelite."* Searching the area for the object, whatever had caused this colossal mess was nowhere to be found. Sure of the cosmic importance of what he had found, Marcel loaded up all they could carry and headed back to the base with a quick stop at his house to show his wife and son.

Eleven year old Jesse Jr. saw the extraordinary material laid out of their kitchen floor. His father explained that he was sure what they were looking at were *"pieces of a flying saucer that had crashed and broken apart."* After a time young Marcel then helped box up the pieces and carry them out to the car so his dad could proceed to the base. He never saw them again.

Marcel and Cavitt detailed their account to Colonel William Blanchard early the following morning and as word was relayed up the chain of command to SAC Headquarters it became clear that there was not one but two impact sites concerning the extraterrestrial craft. Evidence suggested that after being struck by lightning close to Brazel's farm in an electrical storm, the craft was partially blown out above the ground then skidded along the field at the Foster Ranch. It somehow managed to climb back into the air and make it over the nearby mountain range for another 125 miles before crashing west of Socorro where the hull and bodies were found off Pine Ridge Road.

Rewarded for his noble efforts of cooperation, by 9 a.m. the following morning Mac Brazel was seized by Army officials and placed in military custody for questioning, his farm surrounded by armed M.P.'s who began a thorough cleanup of the sight.

But the real excitement began at noon when Air Base Public Information Office First Lieutenant Walter Haut, under the instruction of Colonel Blanchard, delivered the official daily press release to both Roswell radio stations as well as its two newspapers. The headline, *RAAF Captures Flying Saucer On Ranch in Roswell Region* would turn out to be one of the definitive news stories of the 20th century.

For a moment anyway.

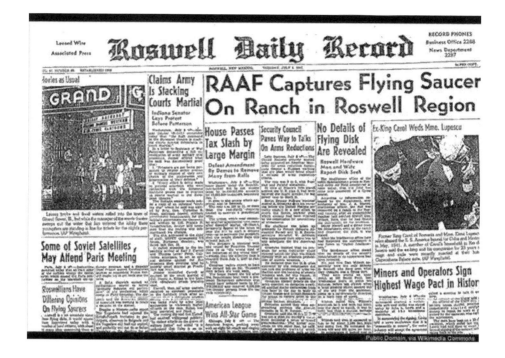

Broadcasted across radio waves within ten minutes, the story began to travel like wildfire and when the news went out over the Associated Press wire at 2:26 that afternoon, a media frenzy quickly ensued with no way of stopping the story. Washington was furious as calls began pouring in from around the country and around the world. The switchboard at Roswell Army Air Base lit up like an over decorated Christmas tree with calls to speak to Blanchard. Avoiding the unexpected hysteria, the colonel and his staff drove out to the Brazel place to personally supervise a company of soldiers with wheelbarrows loading every piece of wreckage into covered trucks. Ordering the wreckage to be placed in possession of Major Marcel, at 3 p.m. he boarded a special flight to Fort Worth Army Base with the debris and ordered to report directly to Brigadier General Roger Ramey. Little did Marcel know that Ramey had received strict orders from Washington to *put out the fire as quickly as possible.* To snuff out the incident using any necessary combination of intimidation and deceit.

The wreckage was taken from Marcel upon his arrival and he was led to the General's office with orders to *"keep quiet and do as told"*. There the floor was strewn with pieces of an old weather balloon, balsa wood sticks and foul smelling burnt rubber. Major Marcel was then ordered to crouch near the pieces while a group of waiting reporters from the *Fort Worth Star* snapped photographs.

The cover-up of the century was underway.

Disk Craze Continues

Army Disk-ounts New Mexico Find As Weather Gear

FORT WORTH, July 9.—(AP)—An examination by the Army revealed last night that a mysterious object found on a lonely New Mexico ranch was a harmless high-altitude weather balloon—not a grounded flying disk.

Excitement was high in disk-conscious Texas until Brig Gen. Roger M. Ramey, commander of the Eight Air Forces with headquarters here cleared up the mystery.

The bundle of tinfoil, broken wood beams and rubber remnants of a balloon was sent here yesterday by army air transport in the wake of reports that it was a flying disk. But the general said the objects were the crushed remains of a Ray wind target used to determine the direction and velocity of winds at high altitudes.

Warrant Officer Irving Newton, forecaster at the Army Air Forces weather station here, said—"we use them because they go much higher than the eye can see."

NOT A FLYING DISC—Major Jesse A. Marcel of Houma, La., intelligence officer of the 509th Bomb Group at Roswell, New Mexico, inspects what was identified by a Fort Worth, Texas, Army Air Base weather forecaster as a ray wind target used to determine the direction and velocity of winds at high altitudes. Initial stories originating from Roswell, where the object was found, had labelled it a "flying disc" but inspection at Fort Worth revealed its true nature. (AP Wirephoto).

LOST PURSE HOLDING DIAMONDS IS FOUND, BUT MONEY MISSING

Somewhere in Corsicana Wed-

At seven p.m. General Ramey held a press conference identifying the fragments as "*Not A Flying Disc*" but a *"high altitude device used by the weather bureau"* and that first reports of a flying saucer were *"incorrect."* Regardless of the Army's desperate attempts to extinguish the truth, ABC's 10 o'clock news Headline *Edition* continued to report the flying disc crash to an audience of nationwide listeners. The evening broadcast even going so far as to state that *"Colonel Blanchard of the Roswell Army Air Base was refusing to give details of what the disc looked like."* Before the broadcast was even finished outraged military officials over the information given by ABC, were on the phone ordering an immediate retraction.

Ordered back to New Mexico from Fort Worth with strict orders to forget what he had seen, Major Marcel was told, *"It's best if you go back to Roswell and forget all of this... we'll handle it from here."*

Knowing what he had picked up was *"no weather balloon and not from this earth,"* Marcel found Captain Cavitt upon his arrival to obtain a copy of the written report from the ranch. Informed he couldn't have it, an angry Marcel snapped, *"I outrank you and I want to see that report!"*

Cavitt simply responded that his orders *"came directly from Washington"* and *"if you don't like it, take it up with them."* Marcel never saw the report.

Even Sheriff Wilcox was threatened by the military in his office with demands to turn over the box of debris he was holding from the Brazel ranch. *"One of the beings did survive the crash"* he was told. Then warned, *"but if you ever talk about it not only would he be killed but they would get the rest of his family as well."* For the rest of his life Wilcox regretted not having called the media to the scene rather than the Army.

As the corrupt Army and Navy began a concentrated campaign to quash the U.F.O. story, the July 9th New Mexico Daily Record headline should have read, *Cover-up of the Century Underway!* but instead announced, *Air Force Declares "Saucer" Weather Balloon.*

Washington delivered a blistering rebuke of the officers in Roswell for causing mass hysteria and under military escort, Mac Brazel was forced to visit the *Roswell Daily Record* who had printed the groundbreaking story and substitute his original account for a carefully rehearsed tale of weather balloons. Making Brazel look like a total fool, when asked why his new version of the incident was significantly different from the one just three days earlier, Brazel replied, *"The military was watching and it would go hard on him if he didn't."* Warning employees of the paper, *"You're better off not knowing anything about it."*

Angry about the encounter at the hospital, Glen Dennis called nurse Naome Self to learn more about what had taken place there. *"It was the most horrible thing I've ever seen in my life,"* she informed. Called in to assist by two doctors whom she'd never seen before, they examined, *"three bodies of a foreign nature"* which she described in detail as having a, *"larger than human head, sunken eyes, small hands with slender fingers and a very peculiar anatomy."* She was shipped out the following day. Ten days later Dennis received a short letter from her with an Army P. O. Box but the follow up letter he sent was returned with a red *DECEASED* stamp and all her military records conveniently vanished.

Newspapers across the country and around the world were slowly forced to accept the Army's explanation of the downed weather balloon and the memory of the historic events that took place in Roswell that fateful summer began to fade. It would be years before anyone would discover that Ramey covered the whole thing up. Not until retired Major Marcel, stewing for three decades over being forced to lie about what he had found, begin telling the real story. Granting interviews to various news organizations, he then publicly admitted that he was indeed, *"the intelligence officer who recovered pieces of the flying saucer that was not from this earth in the summer of 1947."*

His stunning confession re-ignited American interest in the matter and Roswell residence directly involved and living in fear of the government for over 30 years, now in their late 50s and 60s, no longer worried for their safety, were now anxious to tell their stories and expose the truth. UFO enthusiasts from around the world began paying attention.

The rest as they say is history.

******

Chapter 24

Amateurs

1997

Interrupted yet again just as our reporter completes what's been the most interesting account she's ever read, Bonnie reaches toward her night table for the receiver of the ringing telephone and cautiously answers.

"You're a persuasive woman Miss Reynolds." Sheriff Shift's voice bitterly informs.

"Good evening to you too... sheriff." the reporter teases.

"Seems ta me," Shift begins daringly, "you got part of that story you wanted... Would you like to have the other half?"

Eyes open to the bold invitation, "I might..." she replies, still with an air of caution.

"Then do exactly what I say..."

As the agent and his troll watch the reporter's room for any movement or visitors in the seemingly uneventful happenings of the motel parking lot, Bonnie's door opens cautiously as it has several times during the past few hours. Stepping out barefoot a moment later and carrying the ice bucket, this will be her third trip of the evening for a refill. Wearing what appears to be a thin white robe; the reporter leaves her door slightly ajar and heads down the side of the building. Thinking she is out only for a moment on her last ice run of the night, the men stay put.

As Bonnie rounds the corner out of sight, she sheds the bed sheet folded to look like a robe and flings it to her side just as Shift, waiting impatiently by the Coke machine, grabs the woman by the hand. Hardly giving her time to reach inside the ice bucket and fish out her sandals, "Can't you at least let me put my shoes on?" she lightly hisses throwing the bucket to the ground as he begins dragging her along. Forced to hoof it on bare feet, "There's rocks all over this joint!" she complains still clutching the footwear in her hand.

"Welcome to my world." the officer sputters looking forward and marching on. He finds it very difficult at the moment to have any compassion for this vexing femme fatale. She knows it too.

Denny and the boys wait patiently across the street by the old truck parked beside the sheriff's patrol car. Dressed in her bright flowery sundress and now stopped to put on her shoes, Bonnie gives a smile to the three stooges before her. Denny tips his hat politely, Johnny smiles smittenly and Shannon Ray sadly professes, "We got caught."

Unable to hold back a chuckle at his delirium, "So I see," she clowns reaching out to pet the dog whose tail is wagging uncontrollably for his new friend. "You're running with a bunch of amateurs." she whispers to Skeeter just loud enough for all in attendance to hear. The dog lets out a low wine.

"Well..." standing in amusement at the sad looking league of avengers, "the gang's all here..." she jokes turning her attention back to the sheriff, "where to now?"

Chote and Shift exchange concerned glances saying nothing. Each wonders if this really is such a good idea… or not.

"She's been gone too long for ice?" Travers complains after several minutes.

"Did we miss her?" the informant flickers.

Frowning and smouldering for a long moment, "No!" Travers bursts. He grabs the door handle and yanks, exiting the car and marching toward the still open doorway of the journalist's room. The inside is bare except for a brightly colored knapsack lying on the chair with some clothes and things spilling out and an empty pizza box. Propped on a pillow on the bed, seemingly there to draw attention to itself is a book. The agent picks up and reads the title. "Made a fool of again..." he seethes, sending the publication crashing to a corner.

Armed with a couple of shovels and a pick axe from a quick stop at the utility shed behind the sheriff's office, our unsuspecting team walks briskly toward the small Aurora city park. The night had no stars at the moment, hidden by clouds that threatened rain earlier but not delivered. A cool breeze whipped through the shadows causing Bonnie to shiver.

In an effort to catch the reporter up to speed, the sheriff begins, "Decades before anything man made flew over the skies of North America and 50 years before anyone ever heard of Roswell, New Mexico, a similar craft to the one that made history there, crashed here in Aurora. The pilot was buried by order of the sheriff. The reason you couldn' find any headstones goin' back to the 1800s was cause they moved the old town cemetery in 1912. Most'a the markers were nothin' more than wood crosses that had rotted away, so rather than dig up the whole area lookin' fer what bones and graves were scattered about, city officials designated this spot a *"no build"* area which later became the city park."

Entering the grounds, Bonnie and the cousins listen carefully to learn more of the story that brought them together. "When UPI (United Press International) discovered the forgotten legend of a spaceman that crashed in our little town long before it was remotely possible, they released a big news story in 1973 of a Texas cemetery that contained the buried remains of an astronaut who crashed here before the turn of the century."

"In no time UFO hunters were over here armed with shovels and picks and the Feds started snoopin' and askin' all kinda questions, to try and find the grave. After a time things finally settled down then a few years ago the FBI file was handed over to this clown Travers who decided it his number one priority to make a big name for himself by finding the remains. Coming over here, pushin'

folks around and demandin' to know where the body was buried, ol' Clifton led their forensic team all over the countryside, diggin' dozens, if not hundreds of holes for nearly three months."

"Not that old geezer that stormed out of the cafe this morning?" Bonnie questions.

"One in the same." Denny chuckles.

"So what happened?" she asks.

"A Colonel named Alexander over at Carswell, directly involved with the search, realized what a mess this agent had made over here and the amount of money he'd spent, so he had the search called off and saw to it Travers was demoted to a desk job at the FBI. Soon after this same Colonel came over here personally demandin' that if anybody ever came around lookin' for answers that we insist the whole story was all a hoax made up back in the day to save a town that was dyin'.'"

Looking to Johnny as they walk, the sheriff continues, "The wreckage of the silver spaceship from the crash was dumped in an abandoned well on some judge's property and covered over not too long after it happened. So that piece your great papa made off with is the only one left that I know of. Hell, I'd never even seen it before tonight. Heard of it... but never actually seen it."

At the back corner of the park Shift points to an ancient tree, "Our mysterious travelers' buried right over yonder next ta that big live oak."

"So, why the sudden change of heart?" Bonnie asks, "Why tell me all this now after completely skirting me this afternoon?"

"Well damn... dumb and dumber here done showed ya the piece. Before them government sons of bitches roll in here to try and haul him away again, I'd like to get the real story on record, even if we hafta destroy what's left'a him to keep their filthy hands off."

Aurora town cemetery is rumored
...to contain spaceman's body

Hunt goes on
for alien's body

Arriving at the century old burial spot, Denny immediately notices something wrong. "Somebody's been out here diggin'... recently." Far enough from the road to be totally secluded, upon closer inspection the ground has in fact been recently disturbed then haphazardly made to appear like nothing out of the ordinary.

"Surely not Travers?" the sheriff fusses in bemusement before bending down to get a closer look. Touching the ground and feeling several fresh track marks in the dirt, "No..." he corrects, turning toward Denny and shaking his head, "but I think I know who."

Narrow minded with low self esteem, high ambitions and facing an inconsequential life, Michael M. Travers had a tendency to display disturbing signs of defiant and violent behaviour. Feeling that he'd been cheated of his due destiny, anger and resentment smouldered.

A petty thief in his youth, he stole holiday decorations from Long Island neighbors yards for sport, only to discard them after the thrill of the theft had worn away. He killed helpless animals such as gophers and chipmunks just to watch them die and vandalized cars for no other reason than to cause unsuspecting motorists grief. If the true story were to be told, when applying to the bureau he would have never made the cut if it hadn't been for a distinguished high ranking director that was a close family friend. That influence cleared the way for certain "measures" to be taken for his speedy advancement.

Beginning in New York City's, Manhattan fraud division office, he held no credentials in criminology still quickly rising in rank to make a fraternity of enemies in the process. After his soon to be wife, rumoured to have been repeatedly battered by him, suddenly vanished without a trace, he was somehow transferred to Texas with an agent-in-charge position at the Fort Worth office. Three months later he was handed the cold, but nonetheless still open for answers, *Aurora* file.

Incompetent even by FBI standards, he relished for the challenge of confrontation. Eager to prove himself where others had failed, he looked forward to solving the near centuries old mystery by viciously making the residents cooperate, then boasting to all who would listen of his victory. Unfortunately for him, it hadn't quite work out that way.

Sitting on the corner of the bed where Porter had earlier recovered from the shock of seeing a real piece of an alien spaceship, an angry Travers is on the motel telephone. "Yes sir. I know this is not my assignment, but I'm surveying the reporter. People are for whatever reason cooperating with her and I have it on good authority that she's close to discovering crucial details." Failing to mention to his superior the fact that this reporter has given him the slip for a moment, the agent picks up the battered book retrieved from the corner and snidely remarks, "She seems to be committed."

After the exchange and hanging up the phone, "You forgot to mention she gave you the slip there chief." Ralph rubs in with a touch of amusement to the agent's displeasure.

"No one's seen you so far." Travers replies dryly and ready to get rid of him so as not to blow his cover. "Let's keep it that way. Go on home and forget you've seen me. She'll be back... sooner or later..." the corrupt agent continues menacingly, "I'll take it from here."

******

Chapter 25

CryptKeeper

1997

Pulled together now as a dedicated group on a mission, five curious individuals and their dog stand on the front porch of the old home place belonging to none other than Willard Clifton Hawks. Rapping on the door at a few moments past the bewitching hour of midnight, a 12 year old boy, belly down in the living room floor playing video games, looks over at the clock and curses, "Ahhh, shit! This can't be good." His name is Jo.

Clifton's nephew, Jo's dad, Mr. "plantin' flowers or diggin' graves" town caretaker opens the door. "Hmmmm…" he mutters knowing good and well that trouble has indeed arrived, "Might as well come on in…" he invites turning his back and heading inside, "no sense tryin' to stop ya." Yelling back at the uninvited late comers as he moves to the kitchen, "Y'all want some coffee?" then mumbles, "Somethin' tells me it's gonna be a looong night."

Herding inside the entrance room of the near century old farmhouse, the group remains silent as the boy in front of the television continues deep into his game of *Mortal Kombat 3*. Never once looking up, Skeeter goes over and licks him on the face and after making two full circles to find just the right spot, beds down beside the child to watch the animation on the screen.

Pausing in a doorway before the kitchen, nephew bellows, "Uncle! We gots company!" mumbling yet again, "Big troubles, yes sir re baby that's what we got."

"I know that man?" Bonnie says under her breath. Quietly leaning over toward the sheriff, "I talked to him in the cemetery this morning, then saw him loading a truck and watching me at the store where John works when I was talking to the old men out front."

Hobbling into the room with a wide toothless grin, "Howdy folks!" old Clifton yodels hospitably, "Come on in an' set a spell."

Making the connection, "Uncle?" Bonnie quizzes, looking back at the caretaker.

"Yea," he responds, "my grandma's brother married his baby sister and my ma grew up callin' him uncle."

"Me too." Jo injects from the floor. Enthralled in his game but obviously listening to everything said.

"You old fart!" the young reporter scolds the old man, "You deliberately stormed out of the cafe today dismissing all this as 'fairy tales'!"

"Ha!" Jo lets out a laugh. "That's a good one."

Grinning, Clifton hacks, "Time all this is over young lady, you may wished it was."

"Ain't that the truth." spits the boy.

Turning her gaze to the sheriff with a semi nasty look, somewhere between a question and an accusation, the reporter scolds, "You knew?"

Retorting a quick and dry, "Tight community." he dismisses the girl while trying not to laugh at her dilemma and changes the subject back, "Cliff… you know why we're here." It too was somewhere between a question and a statement.

"He knows!" says the boy in the floor. All eyes turn to the youngster who is yet to look up at them.

Taking a seat as the shaggy dog who seemingly loves everyone leaves Jo's side, runs to sit by uncle and puts his paw up for a shake, "Hey Skeeter. How's my boy?" the oldster coos rubbing him on the ear. In no apparent hurry to respond to the sheriff's accusation, Cliff horses with a touch of hostility, "Yea... I know! Y'all barge in here at this hour like the Gestapo!" he chuckles, "I may be old but I ain't ignorant!"

"Nope!" again comes from the floor.

"Where's he at?" Denny asks in his nicest tone.

"In the parlour." the old man hoots.

"In the parlour!" Bonnie screams in shock, covering her mouth with her hand. The action causes Shannon Ray to jump in agitation.

"Oh, yea!" Jo chuckles.

"I knew it." Denny chuckles under his breath as he lowers his head at the craziness of the affair.

Rising from his chair and leading the group into the next room, "Couldn' let the laws get em. Not after all the hell we'd done gone through to keep'em hid."

"Nope!" comes from Jo who pauses the game and is up like lightning and on his feet. No way is he going to miss this.

Entering Clifton's parlour, untouched since Christmas four months prior with several aging holiday trinkets still on shelves and tables, they see a small figure quietly sitting upright in a vintage high back leather chair with tacked buttons on the far side of the room. The child size dehydrated remains of the

100 year old alien traveler still in his burned silver suit. Seated comfortably beneath an antique game board mounted to the wall above, his appearance is similar to that of a shrunken head one may expect to see in a county fair or side show. A multicolour of grey, tan and brown, his flesh has the texture of dried snakeskin with dried up deep hollow eye sockets.

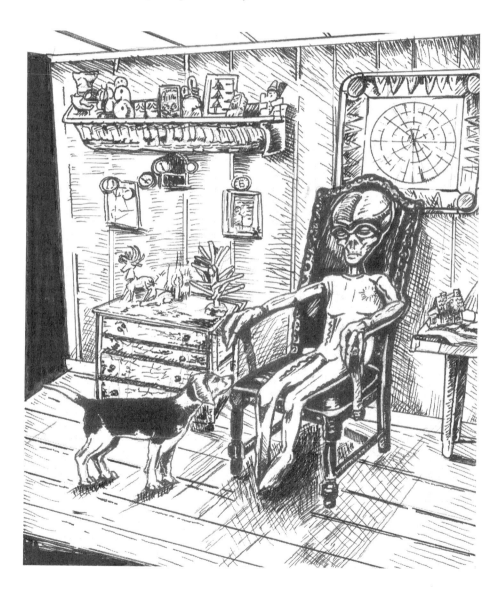

Going down in history as the oddest night of their lives, the group stares in a dropped jaw spectrum of confusion at the bizarre looking little corpse. Her voice reluctant, "Oh-my-God." Bonnie whispers, hand still covering her mouth, then on the heels of that a breathy "I see it but I don't believe it. He looks like the CryptKeeper." Regretting the undignified comparison the moment it came out, in all the evening's astonishment the reference did sort of fit. She was glad though when no one seemed to notice.

"Little bitty thing ain't he?" Shannon comments, "Don't look nothin' a'tall like them critters in them old sci-fi movies on TV. Looks like he's smilin'."

Skeeter runs over and begins sniffing the alien cadaver. Ears swept back against his head, the strange scent crawled up his nose making the fur on his back stiffen. Moving to the dried extraterrestrials side, Clifton zounds, "Oh, he's in fine shape ta be older'n me. This hot dry ground 'round here done dried him out like a big ol' raisin!"

Joining his uncle, Jo brushes away some remaining soil residue from the creature's tiny shoulder and adds, "We cleaned most of the dirt off em before settin' him in the chair," adding with some flair, "Come on over'n touch him. He won't mind!"

As the group moves slightly closer to inspect, Johnny makes a bold move. Knowing Bonnie is shocked by all this he places his hand on her arm and gives it a slight squeeze. Feeling the flutter his touch sends, she turns to face him with a "What the hell have I gotten myself into" look.

The alien's silver suit is still shiny in places, partly melted and heavily stained in others. Clifton takes a seat close to his ancient friend while John and the reporter move to the far side of the room for her to recover her wits from the shock. Hunkered down in the floor beside uncle, Jo stretches Skeeters jaws into smiles and snarls with his fingers for his own amusement. The dog lets the youngster handle him in any old way.

Reaching out to give the dried cadaver a loving pat on the arm, Clifton begins his story of how all this madness came to be. "He was already a legend when I was a boy. I'd go over ta the overgrown cemetery an' put flowers on his grave." continuing on with his recollection, "Don't know why I grew so fond'a the critter, but when they cleared the old cemetery and took up all the markers, I kept his as sorta a souvenir. Back then most'a the markers read "unknown" if some stranger wandered into town and died, but his said TRAVELER.

Determined to conquer this outlandish quagmire a short time later, discussing in hushed tones at Clifton's kitchen table to how and deal with this recent turn of events, Denny and the sheriff put their heads together to spit ball ideas and come up with a feasible plan of action.

"What'n the name'a all that's good and holy are we gonna do with him?" Denny fears, "With them government assholes snoopin' around now, we need to somehow get him away from here. Quick!"

Looking over at Johnny with a tilt and nod of her head, Bonnie takes Johnny by the hand and when no one is paying attention leads him out of the parlour and through the house till they find a back door and slip outside.

"Yea…" Shift agrees with the game warden, "There bound ta be watchin' the roads soon... if not already." Rubbing his chin, contemplating what to do next, "It's a long shot…" he mumbles "but there's one person I know... who might, just might, be able ta help."

Cutting his eyes to Denny in such a way as to make him understand the reference, "Ohhh, HELL NO!" the big man insists. Shuttering at the thought, "We got enough troubles without callin' that crazy fucker in on this!"

"Who else is they we can call? Hmmm?" Shift pleads with agitation. Eyes wide in desperation, "Who else is they we can trust? I mean really trust! If you got a better idea my friend? Now's the time!"

Sometimes darkness can show you the light. Through the cloak of a crepuscule sky, scurrying hand in hand across the dusty landscape of Clifton's moonlit back yard, Bonnie and Johnny make haste in the direction of the farmer's barn. The reporter pulling the young man along the way. Opening and closing the creaking door behind them once inside, the reporter swoops the young man in her arms. Kissing him for several long heartbeats, she becomes lost in her thoughts. Releasing his embrace to take a step back, "I had to get out of there for a while. You okay?" she asks.

"Yea, happy ta be here with you" he admits.

"Me too…" she says seductively pulling the straps of her sundress to the sides and letting it fall as she steps out of it.

Sputtering lightly, "Wowww…" Johnny looks her over as if she were the most astounding creature he's ever laid eyes on. Moonstruck, she had an incredible body with a massive tattoo that swirled from her chest to her side and down one thigh as if she were part wild animal.

Giving him a reassuring wink as she pulls her bra away and tosses it to one side, she waited for what seemed like forever. Standing there in front of this beautiful young man wearing only a smile, her heart was thumping so hard it made her feel almost dizzy. Proudly standing straight, she hoped he would take the initiative to come and grab her up, but he didn't. Just stood there with his eyes dancing her up and down and a look somewhere between astonishment and anticipation.

Lacking the discipline or patience to make him wait, much less herself, the last thing she wanted was to ruin their first intimate moment. She was and forever would be a little sluty and a little dirty but perfectly happy with herself for being that way and didn't know what he may think of her promiscuous past but didn't care, this guy was vastly different. She felt it from the instant she laid eyes on him in that hardware store. Different in so many ways, he was beautiful, innocent and honourable. Anything but naive, she had no doubt he was anything but a virgin several times over. Cocking her head to one side like a confused dog, as her face gains a slight look of amusement, she asks, "Why aren't you undressing?"

******

Chapter 26

Jugs

1997

"Uncle," the sheriff calls to Clifton with the kindest of words, "I might have somewhere we can hide him from them egg suckers. A place they'll never be able ta get their hands on em." Seeing the old man's face light up at the prospect of keeping his buddy save, the sheriff asks, "Just how fragile is he?"

Smacking his lips, Clifton all but squeals, "Why… he's tough as Wilma's beef jerky!"

Shannon makes a painful face recalling "I nearly broke a tooth one time wrestlin' with a piece'a Wilma's jerky."

The sheriff looks to Shannon Ray with a faint smile at his comment, then back to Clifton still hanging out beside the alien as if he were a beloved family member. Still listening to every word but back at his game in front of the TV, young Jo affirms, "Yeah… you can move and bend him like a big ol' Gumby doll." insisting, "He ain't gonna break." Clifton nods and smiles at the sheriff confirming Jo's statement.

"Alright then," Shift chuckles at the sheer craziness of the evening's events, mind made up but still not knowing whether or not his idea is the best course of action, "do you mind if I use your phone?" he asks taking one helluva leap of faith.

"I've never met anyone quite like you before." Bonnie purrs while stroking Johnny's cheek as her gaze runs from side to side of his face.

Brushing the hair from her eyes then running his thumb across her lower lip, he confirms, "Never met nobody like you neither."

She hated any chance of risking what was still such a fresh relationship, then it suddenly dawned on her that she had even considered the pretence "relationship" in her thoughts. That was something the possibility of rarely factored into her thinking. With no doubt of ever growing weary of this boy's face, especially after the behaviour she'd witnessed throughout this extraordinary day and evening, it had been a day she'd certainly never forget in so many ways and it wasn't over yet. His slightly timid hand touched her cheek, soon traveling from her face down to her neck, shoulder and breast which was swelled with excitement.

Nipples more hard and erect than she could remember, his touch found them applying just the right amount of pressure to bring a moan of ecstasy which shot through her like electricity flowing through an open current.

Standing before her and looking into her eyes, he pulled her in for a kiss. His kisses were like nothing she'd experienced before. Heartfelt and a bit shaky at first no doubt due to the unexpectedness of it all, but quickly falling in line with her rhythm. Burning within from his touch, her sex flooded and clenched as her breathing became laboured and ragged. Hot and wet, she throbbed with an irresistible desire to take him for all he was worth.

200 miles away from the unprecedented goings on in Aurora, a Wichita Falls telephone begins to ring at "JUGS" biker bar and strip club.

Dozens of gleaming black "hogs" parked in the lot, several with young prospects standing guard beside them, men covered in black leather and women dressed in not too much of anything, enter and exit. Well past midnight and in full swing, all in attendance complement the appropriate atmosphere of the setting. A dingy dishwater blonde bimbo, seated behind the cash bar with an *I Dream of Jeannie* ponytail and wearing too much make-up, snatches up the receiver to answer the beckoning call, "JUGS!!"

"Yeah…" comes a mild mannered voice on the other end, "lemme speak ta Tombs." Tombs; a.k.a. Wise County Sheriff Shift's only blood brother. A dedicated Texas rebel-rouser and devoted outlaw biker, he couldn't be more opposite than his law upholding brother over in Aurora, but is truly a man who knows how to get shit done.

"Just a sec!" the lollipop cash girl rashes into the phone before tossing it on the counter, annoyed that she has to get her ass up off the stool and search for the bar's owner.

A rockin' Texas band out of Austin is onstage dishing out such "*out of this world*" songs as *Dr. Demon & The Robot Girl, Transylvania Terror Train* and *Redneck Vixen From Outer Space.* Fully enveloped in the live music of *Captain Clegg and the Night Creatures*, the blonde passes several pool games in process then spots Tombs right in the middle of an all nude lap dance by the stage. The place is so packed and so loud everyone has to yell to be heard as she trots over screaming to the top of her lungs, "PHONE!"

Decked out in his club affiliation leather cut, his face and lap filled with naked lady parts, Tombs hair and beard are dark and long and filled with streaks of silver. "WHO THE HELL IS IT?" he thunders, "CAN'T YOU SEE I'M BUSY?"

"I-don't-know!" lollipop screeches back, "All I know is he asked for Tombs!"

Rudely reaching over another man's drink and spilling it on him in the process, the club leader and bar owner snatches up the stage side telephone. Dragging it toward him, grabbing the receiver and holding it to his ear with a belligerent, "WHAT?"

"Answerin' the phone like that," a calm voice teases, "I bet you ain't got too many friends."

"I can't afford friends!" the biker snorts outrageously, "All I got's brothers and mother fuckers that owe me favors! NOW WHICH ONE ARE YOU?"

Standing beside the wall mounted push-button telephone in Clifton's kitchen, his hand propped on the wall above the phone and his head ducked low as he talks, sheriff Shift shakes his head at the "manners" of his sibling, "Nice ta talk ta you too... brother."

Sitting up abruptly at the sudden recognition of his brother's voice, "Andrew?" the bar owner asks with less hostility.

Tossing the nude lap dancer aside with an outlandish, "Move Bitch!" the red headed beauty crashes into the gentleman seated just to the left. More than happy over the intrusion, he latches on to the stripper for dear life and begins fondling and squeezing her all over.

With his black leather bike glove, Tombs covers one ear to hear, oblivious to the squealing and distress directly beside as the redhead struggles to get away. Two bouncers quickly show up to rescue her while harshly dragging Mr. Touchy Feely away and toward the front door, in for one helluva beating when they get him outside.

"What's wrong?" Tombs asks much more humanly this time, his ragged voice now filled with concern.

"What makes ya think somethin's wrong?" the lawman asks with amusement.

"Well!" Tombs fumes, "I can't think a but two reasons you'd call so late on a school night. Either somethin's wrong with mama, or you've got your tit caught'na ringer and none a your tin star buddies can help you out."

"Mama's fine," the brother in Aurora assures enjoying the banter, "but you're partially right."

"Okay then..." Tombs ribs with a grin, "Who'd you shoot?"

"Ain't shot nobody..." Andrew dismisses, turning his gaze toward Shannon Ray for affect, "...not yet anyway. But I do need your help with somethin'. Remember that little feller everybody use to gossip about... the one folks use ta say hadda mishap here and got stranded a-way-way back."

"Yea...?" Tombs questions, remembering the story quite well since childhood.

"Well, believe it or not, he needs a ride outta town."

Rarely lacking for words, the astonished outlaw stills for a moment of contemplation. "You're shittin' me!" he responds, awe struck and unable to believe the little critter in question is "out and about."

In his most serious voice, "No..." Andrew admits, "Not this time."

Considering the request, plotting and scheming for a long moment, wheels are turning inside the bikers head, "How soon?" Tombs questions.

"Now..." comes the answer.

Settling her bra back into place and reaching behind to hook it, covered with a thin layer of sweat despite the chilly night temperatures of early April, Bonnie notices a heavily weathered wooden cross hanging slightly crooked on a bent nail in a far corner of the barn just a few feet from where she stands.

Johnny finishes buttoning his flannel shirt while sneaking a peek at Clifton's seldom seen antique car, a Nassau Blue and Indian Ivory 1956 Chevrolet 210 2-door post, then walks over to politely hand his new friend her sundress. "John..." she says solemnly, motioning toward the old grave marker. As she slips it back on, they both peer through the darkness at the relic, then back to each other with bewildered expressions.

"Well I'll be dang..." he whispers. Taking a few steps for a closer examination, the cross indeed confirms the story in which they heard less than an hour before. An ancient graveyard marker deeply inscribed with a single word...

TRAVELER.

******

Chapter 27

Zombie

1997

Andrew and Denny continue their strategy at the kitchen table as Johnny and Bonnie slip quietly in the back door and through the room. The sheriff gives them an approving wink in passing. Returning a grin of admittance, the reporter has nothing to hide and could care less whatever anybody may think of her business. Johnny on the other hand avoids a direct gaze with either man but has an unmistakeable grin that's impossible to hide... even if he wanted to.

The reporter respects the sheriff more now after all that's transpired and the couple retreat to the couch in the parlour on the far side of the room from their desiccated friend.

"Now how's all this gonna play out?" the sheriff asks his accomplice.

"Well," Denny says, scratching his head in thought, "we could send young missy there back to the motel with a story of how she had to meet somebody with information pertainin' to her questions."

"Yeah, go on…" Shift nods.

Retrieving his rounded pocket size bottle of whiskey, the game warden pours a swig into a small clear glass filled with R.C. Cola and gulps it down as he continues, "First thing that agent's gonna do is rush in there behind her and question as'ta why she slipped out on'em. All she's gotta say is that she was tipped off he was watchin' the room and had to meet an informant that told her 'the thing' she's lookin' for is buried in the park." Raring back slightly in the chair and waving his hands in speculation, the big man prompts, "Chances are, he'll race right over'n check it out while your crazy ass brother's slippin' Mr. Spaceman outta town."

Distracting them, Johnny takes Skeeter out the back door for a much needed break as Bonnie joins Jo, belly down in the floor, to challenge him for a round of his game. They battle fiercely in mortal animation as Jo is thrilled to have an appointment. The reporter is too. As they play Jo's eyes never leave the screen but his stamina for jabbering was unprecedented. He babbles on and on concerning details of the game, how far he'd gotten on different levels and how many times and using which players and...and...and. Seems that the poor kid needs a friend to come over and hang out from time to time... or a dog... or something.

Fast asleep with an eerie drawn look in the chair beside the dehydrated star traveler, with the lights turned low it's difficult to distinguish old Clifton from the recently excavated cadaver, except for the size of course.

Having a moment to mull over the game warden's proposal, the sheriff admits, "I like it, but what if they find those backhoe tracks on the ground same as us. Realize somebody's been up there diggin' in that corner." Shift rubs his hand stressfully back and forth across his chin, "That'd give the whole thing away and we sure don't want em thinkin' somebody else got to him first."

Exhausted and trying unsuccessfully for a quick nap, Shannon has been cautiously quiet during the exchange. Arms folded with his head cradled on the other end of the table, upon hearing a problem in which he can offer a remedy, his head pops up with a solution, "I could fix that iffin I had my big timber back." Noticing the sour reaction from Denny in bring up anything related the morning's events, turning to the sheriff, "Could pack it down nice smooth in no time." Worried that he may have once again said too much, he lays his head back down.

With a slightly evil grin, Shift relishes in the moment, "Ya know, he's right. The two a y'all could clean that spot up in no time. Make it look like it ain't never been touched."

Tossing back another gulp of the mix from his glass, frowning at the remembrance of crashing his Power Wagon into that damn railroad timber a mere 20 hours before, on any given day nothing could convince this man to drive those troublesome brats back out there to retrieve that forsaken thing. But the day had been anything but normal and it would solve their dilemma.

At the ancient traveler's former grave in the upper most corner of the park, following a fast trip to retrieve the lost railroad tie still lying by the side of the gravel road, Shannon Ray slowly drives the old truck back and forth pulling the timber by attached chains, smoothing the earth as the weight of the truck packs it down. On foot, the reluctant game warden puts the finishing touches to the ground, while every now and then nursing his bottle. He expertly adds just the right amount of surface detail to make the recently desicrated gravesite appear undisturbed. Anyone who may come snooping around in this section should be thoroughly convinced the ground hasn't been touched.

Taking in this unexpected spectacle from a short distance, the sheriff asks the reporter, now nestled arm in arm with her new beau, "Ready for your part in all this now?"

Dreading the notion of an all out confrontation with a dastardly federal agent, she replies, "Ready as ever I guess to be interrogated."

"You'll do fine." Johnny reassures with a kind pat.

Placing a hand on each of the couple's shoulders from behind, "Okay then, let's see if we can pull this off." and with a reassuring hint of optimism, the sheriff prompts, "Let's go."

Parked back where they started across the street from the motel and quiet amused by the couple's quick romance, the sheriff looks across the seat of his car at the affectionate pair snuggled closely together. Handing the reporter one of his business cards with Clifton's home phone number written on the back, he instructs, "Now call us out at the farm the minute he's gone… Okay?"

Nodding in agreement, Bonnie kisses John, exits the car and walks in the direction of the motel. Approaching the room, she notices her door, previously left open, now closed and cautiously proceeds to turn the handle. Entering into darkness and reaching for the light switch, frozen in mid step she gasps before being viciously slammed in the face by her own book now in the clutches of the enraged agent.

"Think you can play games with me you little cunt?" Travers menaces at the top of his voice. Knocked to the floor and struggling to get away from her attacker, "Not this time!" he screams crazily striking her head again with all his fury.

Struggling to her knees, hands flailing in an attempt to save her face from another blow. "I found out what you want!" her voice filled with terror, tears streaming, "it's buried in the park!"

"It's buried in the park!," Travers mocks with a high pitched whine, "So I can call in another unit? Be made to look incompetent all over again?"

"NOOOO… I tell you!" the reporter despairs seeing the agent raise the book back to smash her again, "That's where I've been!"

Stopping the attack in mid swing, the agent's eyes open with anticipation of what else she may have to offer.

In a pleading panic, "An informant called this evening and wanted to meet!" she cries, "Told how the town's old cemetery was where the park is now! How everyone around here went out of their way to keep you from it when you were here before!"

Lowering the now mangled book clutched in both hands, the corrupt agent recollects to previous excavations only to realizes that his team never went anywhere near that area. Led all around the countryside in every other direction by that damned old man who conned him into thinking he could assist. He also contemplates that this may be the break he's been looking for all along.

"That's why nothing was ever built on the site!" the girl further informs, "That's where they buried the alien 100 years ago…"

"Who told you all this?" the agent demands.

Defiant to the end and barley back on her feet, Bonnie stands silent.

When no answer comes, the rage returns, "Who told you goddamnit?" he screams just before slamming the ruins of the misshapen book into the side of Bonnie's head like an enraged animal, sending the young lady crashing to the floor and out cold.

Lowering her cigarette to the sounds of screaming and crashing from the adjacent room to the motel office, the attending night clerk doing double duty and not very happy about it, a woman of about 50 with dark hair and long fingernails, looks up from her late night re-run. Riding across the television screen is Jo Nameth on the very zebra striped chopper which inspired Shannon to build the one he's restoring.

She picks up the remote and turns down the sound. Listening on for a brief moment to the savage sounds of an angry man in the next room, she places her half smoked Vantage light in the ashtray and picks up the green rotary desk phone. With a worried look she begins to dial. "Ethel…this is Lorain down at the motel…"

The sheriff's cruiser is about the only car on the road at this time of night as it makes its way out of town. Driving back toward Clifton's farm, "Wonder who coulda' tipped that bastard Travers off so quick ta all this?" the sheriff muses to Johnny.

"Betcha I know!" the cousin quickly insists, "Ralph down at the store. He's the only one heard what me and Bonnie was talkin' about besides her photographer and he wouldn'a done it." frowning with contempt, "He's always come across as kinda shady. Ain't from around here, is he?"

Thinking back, "No…" Shift replies with a slow shake of his head, "No he ain't. Showed up around here not too long after all this shit flared up last time."

As he continues to think back a voice comes over his police band radio, "Base to sheriff…"

Reaching for the mike and responding in an emotionless zombie like voice, "Yeah Ethel, what's up?"

"Sheriff, Lorain from the motel called." Johnny and the sheriff snap looks at each other, "said there's some sorta brawl going on in the room next to her office, come back…"

"Goddammit!" he cringes as emotions boil over. Swerving the police cruiser wildly to the side, he dives to the gravel covered side of the road. Turning around in a cloud of flying dirt the two begin a desperate effort to return to the motel.

Hearing no reply to her message, the office dispatcher's voice once again comes over the waves, "Sheriff? Did you copy?"

Pushing the patrol car to its limit Shift grabs up the microphone,

"ON MY WAY!"

Oozing blood from the corner of her mouth, our reporter lies helpless as Travers leans over her semi-conscious body, pawing and fondling her dress for possible clues. Reaching inside one of the girl's pockets, he retrieves a business card. Gritting his teeth at the thought of this old nemesis, he flips the sheriff's card over to reveal a name and number hand written on the back. *Clifton 814 555 8842.*

Crushing the card, his head filled with thoughts of revenge, "Alright you little trickster!" he rants throwing the card to the floor and snatching up the girl, "You're coming with me!"

*****

Chapter 28

Fight

1997

No rear door handles on the inside and a mesh metal cage separating the front seat from the back of the car, no way Bonnie can escape this back seat prison except to be released from the outside. She was trapped! Unlike Porter's graceful opening of the door for her on his hot 1970 street machine only a few hours before, she'd been literally assaulted, abducted and thrown into the cold vinyl backseat of the black government Ford LTD just as the door slammed almost hitting her yet again. Hair a mess, multiple bruises swelling by the moment and a face that hurt like hell, the taste of her own blood lingered on her tongue from the inner split lip cut open by her teeth. Oh how she wished she could kick this asshole square in the balls.

"Where are we going asshole?" Her insides twisted with deep seated hate as she's bounced in the speeding car. "Where are you taking me?"

"Ahhh, tough bitch now, aye?" Travers seethed, "I told your editor to call off his dog! You should have stuck to covering birthday parties and obituaries back in Gainesville."

Untouched by his sarcasm, "Why are you doing this?" the reporter screams.

His laugh cold as a dead fish, "Because *you* my dear found the secret!"

"I was only doing my job!" Bonnie interjected.

Interrupting with a raised hand, he was finished discussing the matter. No amount of talking was going to do any good with this monster. She'd never been so violated by another human being in her life. Thoughts of revenge flashed for the illegal beating she'd been subjected to. Hearing the agent's bureau issued cellular phone ring through the roar of the racing engine, our hostage listens, "Affirmative! Everything is under control and I've discovered the Aurora Park is the location of the original cemetery. A fact these wretched locals kept from me before. Yes sir, the subject is buried there. I have confirmation." then after a pause, "Yes sir, there's one other lead I need to follow up with before meeting the team but I will be there shortly."

Punching the off button with demonic determination, as they near the farm the injured reporter realizes where they are heading as she hears Travers growl, "Now for that wretched old man."

Checking for the sheriff's card only to find it gone, it becomes clear that this dirty rotten maniac is determined to hurt Mr. Clifton and wreak havoc on anyone who gets in his way. As the speedometer teeters back and forth between 85 and 90 mph, "Still with me baby?" Travers cynically calls out to the back seat.

"Fuck you, mother-fucker!"

"Ohhh, you're fine sugarplum," he laughs, "I didn't figure you'd bruise too easily."

Skidding to a stop in the parking lot of the *Aurora Inn* and finding Miss Reynolds door standing open, the sheriff and Johnny burst inside the room only to realize they're too late. She's gone. Quickly looking around, they see the mangled remains of the book on the floor and beside it a small wadded up piece of paper. Picking it up, the sheriff holds it out to Johnny, "He found the card!"

"With Cliff's name on it..." Johnny remembers.

"We gotta get out there!" Shift confirms as they rush out of the room and back to the car.

Clifton's prized source of transportation is a sharp looking Grabber Blue 1973 Ford F-150 Explorer with white stripes. Purchased new when he sold off several acres of land on the back side of his property that he hadn't stepped foot on in years, the Explorer was Ford's middle of the line model pickup between the cheaper Custom and more expensive XLT. Most of the time the near mint condition pickup sits safely nestled inside the barn but the weather had been so pleasant these first few weeks of April, he had gotten it out to stretch its legs.

Bumping across the gravel driveway with Denny behind the wheel, grandpa Vicker's Dodge comes to a halt beside Cliff''s blue Ford parked to the side in front of the house. Exhausted, Shannon wastes no time getting off the hard metal bucket. Moving through the yard and up the front porch stairs with no words, he disappears inside the screen door.

Denny on the other hand takes his time leaving the driver's seat. Retrieving the bottle that's been keeping him company all night as he steps out, he turns it up for the last time draining the final drops of its contents. Pitching it into the back of the cousin's old truck, he props on the tailgate with one foot on the bumper and lights a much needed Marlboro to relax. "Whatta day..." he exasperates, hopeful that this chaos is nearly over. Soon to be a closed mouth memory.

Finishing the smoke and throwing the butt to the ground, Denny heads toward the porch, making it almost to the top step before hearing the sound of a fast approaching vehicle. As headlights of a black Ford LTD come closer and the car comes into view the game warden realizes his hopefulness is shattered, rumbling a low, "Oh hell... we're fucked now." at the realization that this is not anyone who may possibly be on their side. Quite the opposite, their worst nightmare has arrived.

Lurching to a stop, Travers teases the reporter, "Now you sit here and be a good little girl."

"Bastard!" Bonnie growls.

Seeing the chance to antagonize an old foe, the agent starts in on the game warden as soon as his feet touch the dirt, "Well isn't this cosy! First the over eager newsgirl with your conspirator's card in her pocket. Now the fearless forest ranger babysitting the very piece a shit old man who cost me my job!"

Not knowing that the reporter is helplessly locked in the rear of the car, Denny's look is fierce enough to frighten even a wolverine, "Where's the girl?"

"In my custody." the agent brags, "But with quite a headache I suppose. Her ripe cooch is a bit young for an old brute like you, don't you think?" he taunts walking toward the house, "Little kitten's going to suffer until I get what I want."

The big man tenses, brown eyes narrowed, "Why you..." forming ham size hands into massive fists.

"Uh-uh-uh careful there Smokey..." the agent continues, "better watch what you say. I'm still with the bureau even though you helped these clowns put me behind a desk. Not for much longer!" he insists holding up a finger.

"Cracking this case is just the thing I needed to restore my rank as top field agent in the region."

"Top asshole's more like it." Denny responds.

Reaching the bottom porch step, Travers starts up toward Denny who is purposefully blocking the way, "Out of my way Chote!"

Having about all of this he can stand, Denny rears back quickly as the agent reaches to push him aside and swinging with all his might delivers a crushing blow to his face. The impact stuns the despicable man and catapults him off the steps and to the ground.

Shaking off the blow as best he can, "Good call game warden..." he seethes wiping a thin stream of blood trickling from his nose with the sleeve of his cheap black suit, "Assaulting a Federal agent! Now you can join Miss. pussycat in prison for a few years while this detestable town pays dearly for the humiliation it's caused me!"

From the locked confinement of the black government sedan, Bonnie can see and hear all that is taking place. Problem is she's totally helpless to do anything but watch. And as if that's not bad enough, she has to pee.

Stalking down the steps, Denny has the look of a threatened animal ready to charge its enemy to protect itself no matter what the cost. Retreating a step backwards, "It's not like you can stop me!" Travers boasts a bit less assuredly, "This is only going to make matters worse for you Chote!" backing another step, "I know about the park! A team's already on its way and no matter what you do I'm going to drag this no good farmer" he points toward the house, "up there and grind his nose in the dirt until he shows me EXACTLY WHERE IT IS!"

It's been quite the unforgettable night. Greatly enjoyed and sure to be remembered for the rest of his life, relentless at his game in front of the nine year old Sony TV, Jo has taken full advantage of ignoring his regular bedtime playing round after round of *Mortal Kombat 3*. Left behind from the last excursion, Skeeter perks his head up from Jo's side to troubling noises. Trotting to the window, something outside has alerted the canine. Rearing up on his hind legs, he growls and paws at the window. Pausing the game to investigate, Jo flips the curtain aside to see the big game warden walking toward an unfamiliar man in a black suit.

A super hero taking flight couldn't have done a better job. Half drunk, fully cranked and extremely pissed off, Denny charges the man like an angry bull. Knocking the agent to the ground, he begins pounding him as the two men exchange blows in front of the black Ford.

"Fight!" the boy screams from the window. His eyes grow big to the scene going on in his front yard. Life around here is pretty boring most of the time, running from the window to fetch help, today has been anything but.

The game warden drives a vicious punch straight into the agent's gut that drives the air from his lungs. Fighting to draw a breath, Travers rolls and manages to get to his feet, turn and deliver a smashing blow to Denny's face. Staggering backward, lip crushed and mouth bleeding, Denny swings a right cross which misses its mark. Dodging the blow and hooking a lucky right into Denny's ribs, it sends him sinking to his knees. A hard uppercut to the chin and it looked like Denny may be going down for the count, but instead drove his head into the agent's stomach jack-knifing him to the ground as the men roll in front of Cliff's pretty blue truck.

Now on top, Denny pounds Travers' face with blow after blow. Kicking and snarling in the dirt, the agent's head thrashes from side to side until spotting a decent size stick just out of arm's reach. Pulling all his efforts together into one great arch to jostle Denny's weight, he lunges, reaching for the makeshift wooden club. Fingers clawing, grasping it finally, he brings it up hard and fast smashing Denny in the side of the temple. Spinning to the ground, writhing in pain, blood beginning to run from the game warden's mouth and nose, the agent stands over yet another victim as if trying to decide what to do.

Killing came easy for him; he'd done it before with no remorse. Raising the stick to deliver a deadly blow, it was beginning to look like Denny Chote was done for.

******

Chapter 29

Houston

1997

"BOOM!!!!!!!"

The blast of a 12 gauge shotgun explodes in the still night air. On the front porch with the still smoking Remington pointed toward Travers, stands old Clifton in a rage. "Hyaaat!!! God Dammit that's enough a that shit!" he yells, "Get your ass off my property!"

Jolted from his repose by Jo's cry of a brawl outside, Shannon raced to the window to see for himself. He had managed to doze off on the couch in the corner of the parlour opposite the long dried extraterrestrial and curled up for a much needed nap. Hearing the gun blast and the old man's ultimatum, he and Jo now watch cheek to cheek through the clouded glass panes as they see the agent draw his service weapon. Absorbing the severity of the scene and deciding the situation is rapidly getting out of hand; Shannon leaves the boy's side in a run and races toward the back of the house and out the door.

"Put down the gun!" the corrupt agent commands. Holding his semi automatic, so far concealed in the holster under his jacket in one hand, the makeshift beating stick in the other over a still stunned Denny who's trying with little success to get back on his feet, Travers orders, "You're coming with me old man!"

Weaving his way down the steps with the scattergun still pointed, Clifton snarls, "You dirty rotten pig fucker!"

"That's tellin' him uncle!" Jo cheers from inside.

"I said fer you ta get!" the old man continues, "Ain't nobody goin' nowheres with the likes a you!"

The front screen door bursts open and out of the house with a loaded deer rifle comes nephew Clarence, ready for all out war.

Pointing the service weapon at uncle's chest, "I said put down that gun old man!" Travers demands once more, "and that goes for your accomplice on the porch too!"

Creeping silently with the stealth of a white-tailed buck around the side of the house, Shannon makes his way to the door of his truck. Cautiously opening it, he remains silent and watches the scene unfold.

Unafraid, Clifton starts toward the agent with the gun still aimed. "Whatta you gonna do asshole... shoot me?"

"If the situation demands I will." Travers acting tough begins to worry. Two guns on him from hostiles who hate him almost as much as he hates them. Not to mention the game warden who's just back on his feet and the girl screaming from inside the car. He's put him in a situation that demands an edge.

Still a bit wobbly with his hands to the sides and making no sudden movements, Denny suggests in a gravelly voice, "Why don't you leave that girl and get outta here 'fore you do somethin' you'll regret?"

Considering the game warden's proposal for a quick second, Travers breaks into an evil grin. Suddenly he switches direction of the glock from Clifton's chest to Denny's head.

"Oh, shit!" Jo chokes from the window, Skeeter by his side peering out.

"No you irritating bastard!" Travers begins, turning to the old man with a voice of sinister amusement, "You probably don't care one way or another if you live or die. But I bet you'd hate like hell to watch me kill your keeper here right in front of you." then with a slight head tilt, "Wouldn't you?"

Clifton wobbles, mouth slightly open with a dreadful look of fear, clearly affected by this most recent turn of events, it's as if he's to stunned to move. On the porch nephew inches his vintage gold trigger 30-30 a hair to the right to sight a clean shot and tightens his finger.

With the assurance he has won, the agent warns cocking the hammer back with a promise of fulfilment, "Last chance…"

"POW!!!!!!!!" A flash of deadly neon fire splits the darkness as a second deafening shot rings out gripping the quiet night. The bullet may as well have been a cannon ball. The agent's head exploding in a cloud of red mist. Its backside blown away in a burst of a million little pieces as his body is ratcheted backwards to the dirt. His 9mm falling harmlessly to the ground.

Jo cheers from inside and punches his fist to the ceiling as he turns and does a victory dance. The dog, although unaware of why, dances with him.

Speeding and swerving up the caliche driveway, a muzzle flash is seen and heard from the short distance by Johnny and the sheriff. "Noooo…" a terror filled Shift gasps. Grinding to a cloud filled stop with a look of horror, the two pile out of the car as the shooter lowers his gun.

Among screams from the reporter trapped inside the car, Denny and Clifton look in the direction from which the shot rang. Not from nephew on the front porch, but from the still smoking barrel of Shannon Ray's rifle. The young man who just saved Denny's life.

Beating on the rear door window to be freed; John races to open the door and swoops the girl into his arms as she sobs. Jo walks outside onto the porch and stands beside his dad who rests his hand on the young boy's shoulder. The dog got left inside.

Visibly shaken, "I woudn'a done it cept he pulled that hammer back and then it was too late." Shannon Ray confesses in a low voice.

The sheriff turns his gaze to his friend as the big man confirms, "Two seconds more'n he would'a killed me."

"Shore would'a!" Jo yells from the porch as eyes turn to him, "I seen it!"

"I saw it too." a now slightly less hysterical Bonnie confirms what she witnesses from her confinement only five feet away.

Sheriff Shift takes a deep cleansing breath to survey the shootout. Denny beaten and bloody. The reporter, who appears to have also fought for her life. Uncle Clifton with the 12 gauge. Nephew on the porch with a second gun. Shannon Ray with the rifle now thrown on his shoulder. And a dead federal agent on the ground with the biggest part of his head gone.

"Holy molasses…all this over a hundred year old dried up spaceman." the sheriff muses.

As the welcome rumble of multiple motorcycles becomes clear, "Looks like the cavalry's here." Denny encourages, hobbling to the sheriff's side.

"And not a minute too soon." Shift says almost in a trance. Rubbing his fingers to his aching temple, the lawman turns to the reporter and in an almost accusatory tone scolds, "So…you gonna print all *this*... in your story?"

Shaking her head, "My mama told me if I didn't have anything nice to say... to keep my mouth shut." and with that gives the sheriff a crooked smile and a wink.

Bright flickering headlamps from no less than a dozen glistening black Harley-Davidson motorcycles arrive on the scene forming a semicircle. The roar of the choppers drowns out all talk until the last one is switched off. Silence, but for the popping and cracking of hot exhaust pipes cooling in the night air.

The leader of the pack crawls off his bike first, as is the respected custom. Although from different worlds, respect still runs high among the Shift brothers. Dressed in full black biker garb, totally unmoved by the bizarre surroundings, Tombs steps forward to shake his brother's hand. Not in the traditional way, but in the pagan way of gripping the wrists and forearms. Standing 5 foot 10 inches his boots with a 35 inch waist and 187 pounds, the long haired hellion rasps with a faint smile, "Been awhile... brother."

"Too long." the sheriff agrees, truly delighted to see his kin. "You gonna go by and see mama on your way back through?"

"Thought about it?" Tombs replies precariously, all traces of the smile now gone. "Although I'm still pickin' birdshot outta my ass from the last time I showed up unannounced."

"I remember." Andrew recalls playfully. "But in mama's defence, you don't look much like you did when you first got outta the Navy."

"She still got that mangy ol' cat?" the biker asks with a look of devilment.

"Funny you should mention that..." the sheriff replies, rubbing his chin with a smirk, "Damn thang disappeared 'bout the time you left after she shot atcha. She shore misses that nasty varmint. Couldn' be no connection?" The brothers give each other one last teasing smile before changing the subject.

Looking around, his eyes filled with craziness, "Ain't been to a party like this since I was in Houston!" Tombs booms with a chuckle. Tough as woodpecker lips, his voice animated and raspy, it sounds almost like Michael Keaton's performance of Beetlejuice. Now giving his best performance, Tombs acts a lot like the devious ghost too for that matter. With a proud frown and dreadfully sorry that they missed all the action, he fusses, "You told me ya diddn' shoot nobody!"

"We hadden'… then," the sheriff replies looking toward Shannon Ray, "that was earlier."

Making his way over to the bleeding game warden, "Get caught stealin' girl scout cookies again ranger?" the biker jokes.

Red-faced and split lipped, but otherwise not too much worse for ware, other than a little blood spatter here and there, Denny wisecracks, "I'z doin' all right till that second one jumped in."

Looking at the dead agent with a snarl, Tombs shakes his head vigorously, "Yeah… you gotta watch em! They don't fight fair!" then pointing to the sticky half-dried blood from an ugly gash along Denny's scalp, "Looks like quite a knock there cowboy. If your lucky it'll end up leavin' a nasty little scar."

In his element of expertise, the biker again turns to brother jerking a thumb to the corpse, "So who's the guest of honour?"

"Nosy fed. Been causing a lotta trouble round here for a long time." Andrew replies with a disgusted look toward the corpse.

"Dontcha hate it when that happens." truly enjoying himself, Tombs blasts, "Well you damn sure cured that problem! He won't cause no more! Whatcha gonna do with em?"

Smiling and wincing at the pain of his traumatized head, Denny can't resist teasing, "Aren't you supposed ta know how'ta deal with that sorta thing?"

Tugging at his black jeans and bowing up as if for a fight, "It'd be a whole lot easier to move the damn thing around if it had a head on it!" Throwing his arms up like a true showman and standing tall to take charge of a situation, Tombs outrageously grumbles, "ain't like we can prop the bastard up in the front seat of a car like he was sleepin'!"

******

Chapter 30

Battered

1997

Tear streaked eyeliner gave Bonnie the unmistakable look of a character from the *Rocky Horror Picture Show*. Her face and cheek battered and swollen "I'm all right," she replies as her new companion asks if she's feeling a tad better. Holding up a throbbing hand with once smooth black painted nails now scratched and chipped. "I had to reset this finger," then swishing her tongue around in her mouth, "but I still have all my teeth." cracking a faint smile, she insists, "So, that's a good thing!"

"Shore was worried when we got there and found you gone." John professes.

"How did you know he'd taken me?" she asks.

"Came over the police car radio there was trouble at the motel." he replies, "Woman at the front desk heard the commotion and called it in."

Overhearing the outlandish talk coming from the newcomer, she snickers and covers her mouth taking a look at the obscene black t-shirt this crazy man is wearing, *Ten Million Battered Women In The World But I Still Eat Mine Plain!*

"That's… the sheriff's brother?" she asks in a fog of disbelief.

"Oh yeah…" Johnny replies with a smile, looking at the take charge biker with the idolization of a superstar. "He's great!"

Rubbing a gloved hand on the lower section of his thickly bearded face, Tombs announces the solution to the problem of the cadaver formerly known as Agent Travers. "We'll hafta cut the wind outta him and weight him down good. Then throw him out in the deepest part of the lake, over by the dam." nodding his head to the decision, he satisfactorily concludes, "He'll be fish food in no time!"

Looking to his brother for approval Andrew only tilts his head and looks innocently down as if to signal he has no better idea. With a silent move to two fellow riders accompanying him, they take hold of the corpse without a word dragging it away to do as their leader prescribed. One problem solved and moving right on to the next, Tombs asks, "What about his car?"

Chiming in, Denny informs in a low rasp, "Said he'd done called in a diggin' team to show up at the park."

"He did." Bonnie injects to clarify the facts, "They're supposed to be meeting him there."

Dancing a little jig in the direction of the reporter, Tombs smiles his most charming smile to the pretty young lady as she looks at him as he were indeed Beetlejuice came to life. "Okay darlin…" taking a bow as if asking her to dance, "We'll take his car on over before they get there. Leave the door open with the key in the switch. Run it up on a curb or a rock or somethin'. Make it look like the cocksucker flew outta there in a hurry."

Almost on cue the sheriff finishes the thought with, "As if he was needin' like hell ta get away from somethin'…"

Looking to Denny for his thoughts to the idea, "Why not?" he shrugs.

Tombs points two fingers at a different pair of riders who instantly begin the task. Giving his brother a nod of acknowledgement that it's taken care of, Tombs moves over to the side of a clearly disturbed Shannon and in a thoughtful tone asks, "You all right boy?"

Shannon sadly nods to the affirmative, "Guess I'm goin' ta hell fer this, huh?"

Knowing how to break the tension, Tombs shakes his head vigorously, "Naaa, I betcha it'll be full up long 'fore you and me get there." then inquires to the boy who unbeknownst to the sheriff and Denny he knows extremely well, "Chappa do a good job on your fuel tank?"

Perking right up with a fresh grin, Shannon boasts, "Just like *C.C. & Company*. Ol' Joe'd be proud!" Following the reference to Joe Namath, not considering the others gathered within hearing distance, he adds "And them fancy new scales ya sent works perfect!"

Denny and Andrew cast curious looks at one another. Throwing his hands on his hips in the stance of a lawman, "Since when do you boys need fancy scales for weighin' hay?" clearly not happy that the cousins are growing marijuana for his brother, "Sellin' it by the pound now are ya?"

Loving every minute of this, Tombs is delighted by the perception, "You gonna arrest em.... Sheriff?" he ribs before letting out a hearty laugh. "Haaaa! You really thought they made a livin' sellin' goats... did ya?"

Feeling quite better, Bonnie looks at Johnny with wide eyes. With the realization that her new friend not only works for this wild man, but grows dope for him as well, she smacks him affectionately on the shoulder then once again takes his hand, squeezing it harder than ever.

Problems outside now handled, Tombs smacks his hands together, "Okay, boys and girls... time's a wastin! Where's the little critter we come for?"

Making his way up the front porch steps, Jo examines the biker with the admiration of an ancient god. As if Odin himself had suddenly appeared from Asgard and heading for his front door.

Clifton on the other hand has a different view, almost cowering at the long haired biker entering his home. Noticing the concern before going in Andrew intervenes, "Uncle... you remember my brother?"

Perking his head up to examining the man closer, "Harvey?" the oldster rattles.

"Shhhh...!!!" Tombs shushes impulsively whispering, "Don't call me that out loud." but the damage is done. Tombs right hand man, Buddha, all 400 pounds of him, hears.

Repeating with amusement, "Harvey?"

"So help me..." the leader threatens, "It may take me a whole day! But I'll gut your fat ass worsen that bastard outside if you ever repeat that!"

Buddha smiles an evil smile.

Greatly relieved and now overjoyed to see the long lost Shift brother, "Why-I-do-declare!" Uncle yodels in his elderly tone, "Id'a never known ya under all them whiskers! Come on inside!"

Disappearing in the doorway, "Skeeter! What'a you doin' over here?" Tombs booming voice can clearly be heard talking to the dog, "They got you involved in all this too? Shame on em!"

Seldom rattled, even the great Tombs is a tad put back as they enter the old man's parlour. The ancient aliens dried remains resting comfortably in an antique chair is a sight to make even the strongest of men pause. Leaning toward his brother who is obviously taken aback, the sheriff can't help but tease, "Betcha' never thought you'd live ta see the day?"

"Not hardly." Tombs concurs.

Skeeter runs to sit by the creature's foot like an old friend as Tombs folds his arms and turns to his big accomplice, "Glad we brought that little outfit. He'd stick out in them nasty silver duds."

As the outlaw takes a few steps closer to inspect, Jo folds his arms in a similar manner to mimic his new idol. With still a few pieces of the puzzle yet missing, the pack leader turns to the boy, "Got a black t-shirt?"

"Sure!" the young man yells, anxious to be of any assistance.

With a wink, "Need ta borrow it." Tombs prompts. In a similar manner as the dog had earlier, Tombs leans forward to sniff the creature face to face as Jo runs out of the room. Looking up and over to the left of the shelf filled with Christmas trinkets which have not yet been put away, he notices another shelf filled with original World War II Nazi memorabilia.

"Thanks boy!" the leader insists when Jo runs back in the room handing over the shirt. Holding it up for inspection, there's an iconic image of Bela Lugosi's head as Haitian Bokor, Murder Legendre in the 1932 classic *White Zombie*. "This'll do just fine." the bike leader congratulates.

Walking over for a closer look at the vintage War shelf, among the German conflict items he spies a small Gestapo parade helmet, still intact with the spike on top. Carefully picking it up with a sly grin, he motions the relic toward the old man, "Need to borrow this too…"

A shiny parade of rumbling choppers, lead by none other than the great Tombs, growl their way through the town of Aurora just as the sun appears creeping over the horizon. Cruising past the city park, it is now crowded with a swarm of federal agents along with several archaeologists and a truck load of excavation equipment. Multiple dig sites are being set up under tents and ran up on a big rock sits agent Travers car, surrounded by a string of yellow crime scene tape.

Perfect Strangers by Deep Purple comes over the tiny speaker of Buddha's chopper radio as he cruises behind ape hanger handlebars atop his custom Harley-Davidson. Riding behind the giant man in the "*bitch*" seat is our long lost alien traveler. Dressed in child size leathers over the *White Zombie* t-shirt, his tiny gloved hands are discreetly held to the small armrests with black electrical tape.

Fully accessorized with wide mirrored sun shades and Clifton's old Nazi helmet strapped in place, they roll pass the park. Head tilted in the direction which he rested for nearly 100 years, if one didn't know any better... they would swear the youngster was, "smilin" in the sunshine and enjoying the ride.

******

Conclusion

The feds found and excavated about 30 unmarked graves dating all the way back to the Civil War. None of which turned out to be the one they were looking for. After nearly destroying the park they finally stamped the case, "CLOSED." No one ever so much as mentioned agent Travers.

Inside a very private and protected organization lead by none other than Tombs himself, our mysterious traveler found himself a safe place to stay. At the end of the biker clubs fraternal meeting table sits a special seat, a throne occupied by none other than the dehydrated traveler. Still dressed in black and wearing an honorary cut, he became master of the throne and overseer of the table in an organization where silence is not only golden... but mandatory!

Although edited for content Miss Reynolds got to write her story which added a new twist to an old legend. Airing on the side of caution toward those she had befriended, to have written it in its entirety would have most assuredly won her national recognition, but at the same time may have possibly won poor Shannon Ray a death sentence.

A Century In The News

By Bonnie Reynolds

April 17, 1997

In 1897, a traveler from the sky was blown off course. He crashed into a windmill and water tower in the nearby town of Aurora and perished. The pilot of the downed craft removed from the wreckage was said by witnesses to be a small being with a large head and "*not an inhabitant of this world.*" A United States Signal Service officer at the scene going so far as to report, "*in my opinion the pilot is a native of the planet Mars.*"

Local inhabitants of the time did what they could for this creature, the same they would have done for one of their own or anyone else who may have wondered into town and died. They carefully placed him in a handmade coffin and laid him to rest in their town cemetery with full Christian rites. Taking place during a rash of unexplained "airship" sightings between 1895 and 1898, eyewitnesses of the time described flying machines constructed of a metal resembling a mixture of aluminium and silver which produced blinding flashes of light.

Whether or not the unfortunate traveler laid to rest in Aurora was indeed "*not of this world*" remains uncertain. But what is certain is that the good people of the time did what they believed was their civic and righteous duty. To give the stranded traveler a decent burial.

After spending a few days with several of Aurora's current residents, I can't say for certainty where the final resting place of the mysterious traveler is located, but what I can say is that I found a community with the same dignity and integrity as its ancestors had 100 years ago.

******

The Author

A devoted antique car collector, judge and restorer for the better part of 25 years, Kerry Trent Haggard is the founder, writer and host of "Wheels of the Past" productions based in Beaver Falls, PA. Relocating there to begin the project from his home state of Georgia in 2017, currently under production in the Pittsburgh area, "Wheels of the Past" is a historically accurate and entertaining series devoted to the history and preservation of classic cars, trucks and motorcycles which have informative stories to tell.

Working as company buyer for SMS Auto Fabrics of Canby Oregon from 1989 till the mid 2000s, Haggard personally built several national award winning AACA and Early V-8 show cars including a 1924 Ford Model T Touring car, 1961 Ford Galaxie Starliner and a 1938 Ford DeLuxe Coupe which won "Best Pre WWII Ford in the Nation" in 2000.

A long time enthusiast of classic horror and UFOs, Kerry first learned of the Aurora alien crash from friend and Texas native John Cochran in the summer of 2015. Due to an incident which Kerry witnessed during his childhood of a flying saucer landing in his small hometown, the story hit him with such passion that he and John spent the next several months working day and night to form an outline for a screenplay based on the fictional hunt for the buried extraterrestrial 100 years later. From there it grew into the novel you are holding. Bonnie's editor Mr. Grail in the story is based on Kerry and the young boy Jo, on his grandson Kane.

The Co-Author

Born July 14th 1970 in Odessa Texas the real Johnny Cochran from whom much of this story is based, including not only the Johnny character but Tombs as well, was raised in the country and grew up hunting and fishing and working as a rough and rowdy cowboy on local ranches.

Graduating from Permian High School in 1988, he joined the United States Navy and became a corpsman serving his term with an honourable discharge. Following his stint in the Navy, he came home to West Texas to work in the oil fields where he now owns two successful businesses, an oil field supply company and an on location mechanic outfit.

Through his businesses he has made many acquaintances, a few he calls friends and a select number that he considers Brothers. The father of six beautiful children, family and honour have always been of the utmost importance. With a lifelong love for old hot rods and motorcycles, John is a true friend, a free spirit and always up for a road trip.

The Illustrator

Illustrator and canvas painter, Eric Yates is an antique collector and picker. Other creative outlets are music and vintage cars. In his youth he would strip cars for scrap at junkyard. He would also draw portraits and the comic hero "Conan the Barbarian". Graduating 1990 from the Art Institute of Atlanta, he earned a degree in illustration and graphic design. During school he freelanced, drawing characters for "Gillette Razors" and also painted mannequin faces among other freelance for clients. In 1991-1992 he was a substitute teacher at Elizabethtown Community College where he taught graphic design and did graphic art for Chamber of Commerce and the College. In 1992 he studied architecture and vintage paintings in Lucca and Pisa Italy. In 1993 he went back to his roots illustrating fantasy sci-fi and horror art. From 1993-2005 attended cons and art shows in many states. Selling originals and making prints. 1998 won "Best Horror" award in River Con Art Show Louisville Ky. In 1999 won third place "Mid South award". Continuing art shows and painting, creating original ideas. In 2005 won "Best in Show" at Conglomeration in Louisville Ky. Continuing Art Shows throughout and selling prints of his oil paintings. While selling prints at art shows decided to experiment airbrush on automotive vehicles. 2006 began car shows winning trophies. 2010 winning "Best Compact" at Carl Capers Custom Art show in Louisville and also again in 2017. Currently still attending art shows, painting originals and selling prints.

The Editor

A professional educator for 15 years, Carla Ricci is currently employed as an elementary art teacher near Athens, Georgia. Having a passion for creativity and children, she shares her ideas and knowledge with kids aged 5-11. She is also a mother and reader with a fascination for all things alien. The story of Aurora was brought to her through a documentary that grabbed her attention and from then it was a knowledge hunt. Taking on the roll of editor, she worked closely on the novel after Haggard introduced her to it.

In addition I would like to express my sincere thanks to the following:

Bonnie Calnek of Portland OR, who the Bonnie character is loosely based.

Shannon Hoffman of St. Petersburg FL, who the Shannon Ray character is based.

Noe Torres for helpful information in his book "Real Cowboys And Aliens Of The Old West".

Kevin Randle and Donald Schmitt for their book "Truth About The UFO Crash At Roswell".

Plus: a special thanks to Lynn Davidson, Mark Randall, Philip Mantle, Robert Snow, Georgette Frey, Michael Staaf, Betsy Elliott, & Doc Herndon.

As well as the late Denny Chote, William Johnstone, Bela Lugosi, Boris Karloff, Lon Chaney Jr., Darren McGavin, Rod Taylor and Henry Ford for their inspiring influence.

******

Based on the Aurora, TX alien crash of April 17, 1897

Twenty-four-year-old Gainesville Texas newspaper columnist Bonnie Reynolds has been handed an assignment. Finding the resting place of a 100 year old extraterrestrial buried in the small town of Aurora, Texas. According to local reports published in both Dallas and Fort Worth papers of the time, a small being clipped the local windmill with his silver flying machine and slammed head on into the town's only water tower.

Good-hearted folks of the time realized that he was "not of this world" but did the one thing they could for the fallen traveler. They gave him a proper Christian burial.

The quest to locate his grave turns out to be more than an ordinary newspaper assignment. What she finds is a select few members of the town struggling to keep an ancient secret from corrupt federal agents determined to do harm and by the time its over the reporter wishes she had never seen the ancient article which led her down this road.

That is until an outlaw named Tombs rides in to save the day.

FOR FURTHER BOOKS FROM FLYING DISK PRESS

http://flyingdiskpress.blogspot.co.uk/

Made in the USA
Middletown, DE
26 February 2019